LETTERS TO MOM AND DAD

LETTERS TO MOM AND DAD

And Things That Happened Along the Way

Lucée Santini

For my father, George

Contents (Stories)

Foreword

My mother always said I had a vivid imagination. Whether it was a story about the girl in the woods near our house that got "raked," or the time Margaret Thatcher petted me on the head in a baby contest. I would bring it up years later and she would say "of course that didn't happen, Zoe, what made you think that?"

I swore I visited Oregon when I was ten years old; and, had an altercation with a transvestite in London when I was thirteen. "You've never been to Oregon!" she laughed. Yet my mother always encouraged me to be creative.

This book is a collection of stories loosely based on real events that took place in my life. My perception of the events are through my eyes and are sometimes embellished for the sake of a good laugh, or just the fact that my imagination got the best of me. Names have been changed but the stories and letters that were written are real.

Acknowledgments

This book would not have been possible without the patience and encouragement of my dear husband. Words cannot express the gratitude for my editors, Robin Spillias and Lisa Leppek. Robin, all the time you put in and suggestions are greatly appreciated. Lisa, thank you for forcing me to step out of my comfort zone. Thank you to John Hall Photography and Lissette Raquel Photography. Lastly, thank you to my parents and all my friends who encouraged me and saw potential that sometimes I did not recognize.

HAVE A NICE DAY

02/02/1993
Dear Mom and Dad,
Well, I live in a hotel, if that's what you want to call it. It's more like a dorm. I live in a room with three beds about as big as my room (a little bigger). It has a closet and a balcony, a tiny dressing table and a bathroom. The shower has no door so you can imagine the mess afterwards. But there's a lot of hot water even though Yanni said he had to cut it down because of the new law. He and dad would get along great since he also doesn't believe in heating either. Anyway, it costs 3,500 drachmas to do two loads of washing – that's the cheapest I've found. The hotel is right next to the acropolis in Koukaki. There are lots of markets to get things also. We also have a tiny refrigerator under our microscopic dressing table. And there's a hole that everyone refers to as the kitchen here. You can cook whatever. Lately, my roommate and I have been making macaroni.
Yanni, the owner, is sort of strict. He doesn't like you to wear a bathing suit on the roof and whenever my roommate comes home from her boyfriend's apartment the next morning he always looks at her disapprovingly like he's her father. He also has my passport. I guess everybody in the hotel has to give it to him and he locks them up. He says he has to because they check him out to

1

see if the models are staying longer than they should. They get a three month holiday visa.

I can't believe this is happening. Since I was eight years old, I dreamed of becoming a fashion model. I wonder if I will be here longer than three months...I hope so. Let the journey begin!

Love Zoe

I was eight-years-old when my mom and I stepped off the plane coming from Newport Pagnell, England to embrace the American dream.

We had heard so much about this place called "America." The United States, the land of the free, home of the brave. All my classmates were in awe that I was moving there. I was going to "that" place -- America. They bid me farewell and later sent letters of envy.

I was officially a Yankee, and my British accent was about to be hijacked by an American one. I had heard that the Americans drove sports cars, ate hamburgers and drank beer. Fast cars and beer bellies are what I had to look forward to. *"America is the place where dreams come true,"* rang in my head. We called it the "land of opportunity." On television we saw houses with swimming pools, white picket fences, huge back yards with barbeques, and two-car garages. Everything was super-sized, including the people. Big cars, big yards, and big people. This was the American dream my father had talked about for so many months.

We waited patiently in England for my father to bring us over when the time was right. He had been recruited to work in Long Beach, California. But later was offered a different job in Seattle, Washington which is when he decided to bring us over. We locked up the house in England and put Sophie, our Great Dane, in a kennel. Little did I know that would be the last time I lived in that house, and the last time I saw Sophie. Now, we were about to embark on this American dream that everyone was talking about, and, our life was about to be forever changed.

My father picked us up at the airport and drove us through Seattle. As I looked out the window, wet from the pounding rain, I noticed how green everything was.

"Khristos! It's raining cats and dogs!" my mom said.

It didn't seem too much of a shock to me, this place called "America." The rain was pelting down on the windshield and it felt like we were going through a car wash. The air was damp and the sky was gray with no promise of sunshine.

Am I still in England? I wondered.

After a long trip of flying, we were feeling "a bit peckish," as my mother would often say, and my father took us to a local restaurant. When he ordered steak, my mom was shocked.

"Khristos, can we afford that?" she said in her proper British accent.

She emphasized the "t" at the end of "that" and pulled up her shoulders.

"Of course," my father said in his thick Greek accent while throwing his arms up in the air. He was smiling and nodding his head like he had secret to the *DaVinci Code*. But eating steak was a luxury we could not afford when we lived in England. The only time I remember eating out was for fish and chips. Pizza Hut had just opened in the UK and it was a luxury to dine there, where wine was served and pizza was eaten with a knife and fork.

Our dinners in England consisted more of liver and onions, bangers and mash, and eggs and chips. We had wonderful Sunday dinners where my mother cooked as if she were feeding an army. It was like having a Thanksgiving dinner every Sunday. It was a feast of all feasts that would be an all-day affair, surrounded by family. She would cook roast beef and Yorkshire pudding -- an English tradition. Sometimes we finished it off with her famous apple crumble smothered in brown sugar and heavy cream. By the end of the day, we were all still sitting in front of the "telly" with our pants unzipped complaining how stuffed we were.

After our extravagant steak dinner, we stopped off at a grocery store which felt more like being in a shopping mall. As we walked up to the store, I looked up and saw a big sign that read, "Fred

Meyer." I wondered if he was the owner of this shopping mall.

Who was this Fred Meyer and does he have children; specifically a son about nine years old? I thought.

As I stared at this big red sign displayed on the building I imagined what it was like to be Mrs. Meyer. I envisioned Mr. Meyer sitting on a throne with servants all around, as he counted his millions. This super-sized super market had patio furniture, toys, electronics, food, and much more. I was overwhelmed at the amount of stuff that was available for sale. I had never been to a store where I could buy milk, a television, lipstick, a cassette tape, and silly putty all in one place. Silly putty didn't even exist in England. Nor did the slinky. I made a mental note to come back alone to shop in the toy department when I had some pocket money.

When we checked out, the cashier told us to "have a nice day." My mom and I looked at each other in amazement. Our mouths dropped open, eyebrows furrowed and the look of confusion fell over us. Well, actually my unibrow furrowed and my mom's two remaining brow hairs -- from when she over plucked them in the 60s -- popped straight out. My mom was beautiful with flawless porcelain skin. She had piercing green eyes and blonde hair cut in a bob, with high cheek bones and full lips. Everybody said she looked like Lady Di which was flattering because she adored the Royal Family.

She was in the Royal Navy and was proud to be English. I, on the other hand, resembled my father. I had dark brown, wiry hair, the Greek temper and my Yia Yia's eyes.

Why would this woman care if we had a nice day? What were we supposed to say? Surely she didn't really care how our day would be. But we would later discover that Americans were quite cheery, open, loud and warm people, unlike the Brits, who were reserved and cold (in my eight-year-old opinion). Hugs were few and far between if any. In Greece however, it was much different. I would see my Grandmother and anticipate my cheeks pulled left and right.

"Koukla mou!" my Grandmother would yell in delight with her eyes lit up like sparkling silver stars.

All her friends would come over to play cards, smoke and drink coffee around the kitchen table and I would try not to make eye contact through the cloud of smoke. As soon as they saw me, my cheeks would quiver.

We settled into our little life in our apartment in Everette, savoring all the new types of food. On Sundays, we would go to Winchell's Donut Shop where we would eat apple fritters, and donuts that looked like mini frosted cakes with holes in the middle. They didn't have such a thing in England at the time. Back home, I would wait in line at a farmers market to buy the American "cookies." They had a distinct taste and nothing like the

English biscuits that you dunked in your tea. These cookies were spectacular. They were crispy, sugary, large cookies with pieces of chocolate floating inside them. I would later find out that the chocolate chip cookie was to be dunked in milk and that it didn't dissolve in your mouth like the English tea biscuit or shortbread. You had time to savor and enjoy it. If you waited too long to dunk the English biscuit it would fall apart in the tea and you would have to go fishing for it. This was not an attractive display for a proper English girl.

Saturday mornings were like going on vacation or as the Brits would say "holiday." The American kids I knew ate cereal like Captain Crunch or Fruit Loops and drank strawberry Quik for breakfast. In England, the most exciting cereal we had was called Weetabix. The name itself put a damper on anticipating breakfast and I was better off skipping it. Then there was the endless supply of cartoons: *The Smurfs, Fat Albert, Road Runner, Bugs Bunny,* and the *Care Bears.* At eight years old, Saturday was the only day I would get up at the crack of dawn to watch cartoons. I would sit in front of the television for hours, Indian-style, with my nighty hiked up to my waist and my underwear showing. My eyes would be glued to the television as I ate my Captain Crunch and my mom would say, "Close your legs Zoe, we don't want to see what you've had for breakfast!"

LETTERS TO MOM AND DAD

RUBBISH

The bus picked me up to take me to my first day of third grade. There, I would have many firsts. I would learn cursive handwriting for the first time, have my first Asian boyfriend, and I would pee my pants in public.

It was an adjustment coming from an English school, but I had also moved to Greece when I was seven and went to school there. So, I was accustomed to change. School in general was easier in the United States than it was in England. If I had stayed in England I would have been learning French already. So, I wasn't intimidated by the work load. The teacher gave us an assignment to write in cursive but I had no idea what she was talking about.

What was this "cursive" language? I thought.

Then, I turned in my assignment and she called me back to her desk. She told me I needed to end each sentence with a period.

Period? I thought. *Why would I do that?*

So I wrote out the word "period" at the end of each sentence like a good student and turned it in. She was baffled. She explained that a period was the dot at the end of the sentence and that I had neglected to do it.

AAAAHHHH, a "full stop!" I thought.

This is what we called a "period" in England. And so it would be the first of many language differences I would come across.

I had known about language barriers from an early age when my mom sent me to Greece to spend the summers with my Yia Yia and my cousins. Their first language was French, but they knew a little English and Greek also. So we learned to talk to each other using all three languages. Of course my Grandmother only spoke Greek to us. So when we moved to the States I thought I had reached the limit with the language barriers.

After all English is English, I thought, *it can't be much different in America.*

But I had yet to find out and to be as embarrassed as my father, when he tried to order a hundred "rubbers" from Boeing's office supply store. Specifically, he ordered pink ones because "they do not leave a trace on paper", he said. In England, a rubber is an eraser, not a condom.

Or when my mother said to our neighbor Jim, who called to tell her that he'd lost his job, "so sorry to hear that Jim, keep your pecker up!" She said he seemed a little confused when they got off the phone. "Oh well, what's done is done", she said in her British accent. "It's water under the bridge now."

Besides the language barrier, lunch was also an adjustment for me. The English were definitely more civilized at dining than Americans, and I had a hard time adapting to one of the most important times of the day for me - lunch. We were given our milk in cardboard cartons in which you had to put your finger in between the seal to open it and pull out so that you drank from a V--shaped box.

Why did they give us milk in a carton? How uncivilized, I thought.

The cardboard to my lips felt like chalk on a chalk board. It was like drinking out of a wet box. The milk was watery. This was not like the milk I was accustomed to in England which came in glass bottles, delivered fresh that day, with cream around the edges.

This is rubbish! I thought as my crooked, deviated septum of a British eight-year-old nose turned up.

Gone were the days of scones with jam and Devonshire cream. I already missed my Branston Pickle, cheese and cucumber sandwiches and my salty Marmite. I longed for Smarties and Wine Gums. I missed the ice cream cones that I could get on the streets of London with my Flaky bar inside. I was definitely disappointed in the American cows and their lacking in production of milk. Later they would put missing children on the milk cartons and drinking it became even more depressing. Every day my eight-year-old self would be faced with the state of the world as I contemplated what happened to these poor children.

LETTERS TO MOM AND DAD

JUST LIKE STARTING OVER

After living stateside for a few months, the news reported that John Lennon had been shot. I remember this day clearly, not because John Lennon died, but because I accidentally set my hair on fire.

I had long, wavy, kinky hair and was blow drying it upstairs in my parent's bedroom. I could hear my mom sobbing and remembered that Luke and Laura's wedding day (from *General Hospital*) was approaching and that today must be the day. My mom was downstairs with a box of tissues watching the news, shaking her head.

"I just can't believe it," she cried.

She had been a Beatles fan all her life. She had all their songs memorized, and growing up I would witness Beatlemania as she swung her hips, "Shake it a baby now, shake it a baby, twist and shout, twist and shout......" she sang as she did the "twist" around the house.

I saw smoke coming from the hairdryer and felt my hair get wrapped up inside of it. I screamed at the top of my lungs and unplugged the hair dryer. I ran downstairs with it attached to my hair as the smell of burnt hair engulfed my mom.

"Mom! Mom! My hair's on fire!" I screamed.

She jumped up and helped me cut the hair out of the hair dryer all while keeping another eye on the television. "I just can't believe he's dead," she rambled on and on. "Who would do something like this? Why? Why?" I suppose I could have said the house was on fire and it wouldn't have fazed her on a day like this.

"He's going to prison for life, he is. They're not going to let him get away with this. Didn't someone see it coming?"

She cried as she blew her nose in her 100% cotton hanky all the while asking the same questions as if she could have stopped it from happening.

"So tragic, such a shame, this world has gone barmy you know. You can't trust anybody. Zoe, I worry about you. Don't ever talk to strangers, oh, and make sure you look both ways before crossing the streets," as if it had anything to do with John Lennon dying.

So while avoiding strangers and air drying my hair from then on, just like any third grader, I had my eyes set on a new boy. On the playground all the girls flocked to him like he was Ricky Martin. Whatever it was, he had it: charm, charisma, swagger and all the girl's attention. Wherever he went they followed, like his little disciples. He was tall (as tall as a third grader could get), dark, and handsome. I would have my first Asian boyfriend.

However, the relationship would be short lived due to the fact that half the classroom was dating him. I'm not even sure if we spoke during our brief affair but I wasn't going to be the other woman, so I ended my one day affair with my Asian gigolo boyfriend. This was not a good start to my dating career.

Back in England, I briefly "went with" as they say in America, a young boy named Ian. He was the opposite of the current boyfriend who had black hair. Ian was Irish, had blond hair with blue eyes and a mischievous smile. His idea of a date was meeting me at the park and the both of us peeing in the sand pit or behind the bushes. I guess my standards were low from the very beginning.

Outside on the playground during recess, the kids played this game that was new to me that I quite enjoyed. It involved four people passing a ball around, which was a good start to learning playground games since the only game I knew was hop scotch. During the game something or somebody made me laugh quite hard and I regrettably peed my pants. Horrified, I calmly excused myself and went to the nurse's office.

"Oh dear, what happened?" she asked.

I told her that I had stepped in a puddle and splashed myself. The nurse examined me and looked a little skeptical as it wasn't raining at the time.

"Right......," she said nodding her head.

I was so nervous, but I stood my ground and stuck to my story. She ran her fingers inside the seam of my jeans and said, "Oh, yes, you splashed yourself. Let me call your mom to get her to bring you some fresh clothes."

My mom rushed to my school and dropped off some clean clothes. She was the perfect housewife, cooking and cleaning, folding and ironing making me a casualty of *General Hospital* and *The Young and the Restless*.

As I watched it with her, I never knew so much drama could happen on a daily basis. My life, even with moving to America, suddenly became boring. I would have given up my American dream to go and live with Victor Newman in a heartbeat. My mom would sit in anticipation, biting her lip, waiting for Victor Newman's next big decision as if everything depended on it. Then it would be Friday and we would always be left hanging until Monday and she would let out a big sigh.

I made a couple of friends in the neighborhood. One of them had two fathers which was a foreign concept to me. In England, divorce wasn't popular at that time and so step parents were never talked about.

At least you get more gifts, I thought.

Our next door neighbors came over and they invited us to their church, and it was just a matter of time before my mom was being baptized in a lake. I knew she was serious because she couldn't swim and was afraid of water. I started to go to bible retreats and Sunday school which I quite liked. "Jesus loves me" was the theme song. Church became a regular event, and I quickly realized that this was a good way for me to meet boys. So church became a priority, sometimes three times a week.

Although we spent a lot of time with our neighbors, my father wasn't a big fan of church. So he spent a lot of time working on projects at work like building rocket propellers. He had gotten his PhD in neuroscience and studied explosives -- which explained the problems with the septic tank under his house in Greece. When he was home and not working, he was conjuring up some new experiment on his computer. This time her name was Eliza, the digital girlfriend. He would sit for hours having conversations with her.

"How are you today, Eliza?" He'd ask with his morning coffee and cigarette.

"I am very well Khristos," she would say in her mechanical voice, "how are you today, Khristos?"

I could hear him laughing in his office completely satisfied with what he had just invented while asking her inappropriate questions. And so every morning we woke up to the voice of Eliza, the digital girlfriend.

The questions were endless and soon my dad's computer (which he nicknamed DGS for digital genitals) was getting on my mom's nerves.

"Why don't you like her?" my father would ask.

"Oh Khristos, it's just not my cup of tea," she answered. Until finally she had had enough with Eliza and ordered him to break up with her.

"You've gone barmy," she said, "Do you realize that she's not real?"

"Oh Ellen, calm down, don't get your knickers in a twist!" he'd say, "It's just a game."

So that was the end of his relationship with Eliza. We never spoke of her again.

ON THE ROAD AGAIN

It was just over a year in Seattle when my father was offered a great job in Arizona, so we packed up our treasure and drove to Phoenix. I'd attempt to sleep in the back but my father's blasting Willie Nelson's "On the Road Again" would keep me awake.

It was nothing like Seattle. The sun came out every day, promising sunburns and dehydration. I felt like I had stuck my head in the oven. I was boiling and broiling. The desert was endless and the only green vegetation visible were the cactus plants. I felt the energy get sucked out of me the longer I stayed outside. The ground burnt through my flip flops, my earrings burnt my ears, and my hair resembled a horse's tail. My mom would eventually have to tackle that issue by taking me downtown to the African American men's barber shop to get my hair relaxed. I would leave with beautiful straight silky hair only to come home later and discover scabs all over my head and a headache from all the chemicals. At nine-years-old, I was already learning the price of beauty.

That summer, my father rented a house so that the family from Greece could visit. They had never been to America so now was a good opportunity to fit ten people in a three bedroom house. We needed some furniture so we went on the hunt for some second-hand furniture. We ended up at

Jackson's Used Furniture Store and soon realized that the owner was the father of a famous actress. He gave us a signed photograph of her. I thought after purchasing half of his store that was the least he could do.

I was quite embarrassed as the used furniture truck came to drop off the furniture in our upscale neighborhood. The neighbors didn't know we were only there temporarily. They must have been surprised after watching us move in, to see another family of five move in along with my grandmother and her friend, Eliki. I couldn't wait to play with my cousins. They were close to my age and I didn't know anyone in our new neighborhood.

My mom enrolled us in summer camp which would get us out of the house for a while. We were there to do physical activities and go on field trips, but their idea of a field trip was dropping us off at 7-Eleven to buy slushies and candy. The field trips I envisioned were more like the Grand Canyon. I grew sick of the Nature Valley Granola Bars they doled out to us every day. I saw the green packaging and wanted to run. We lined up and I'd pray that we weren't forced to eat this "healthy snack" we got daily but instead go swimming in the pool.

One day I was swimming at the bottom of the pool, running my hands along the floor and three kids dived right above me, when suddenly I was kicked in the head. I came up above the water with my head spinning, feeling sick, trying to motion to the lifeguard that I was hurt. I suppose there must have been too many drownings that day and he was too busy for me, because he motioned to me to get out on the side steps.

Whose 'life' in the word 'lifeguard' is this job referring to? I thought as I pulled myself out of the water trying to keep my balance from being dizzy.

Then, thankfully I saw my cousin and yelled out to her. She saw that I needed help and helped me walk to an employee. After examining me and determining that I should stay there until my parents picked me up (which is code for "we don't need to get sued"), they took me to the gym and laid me down on the floor. *God forbid I could have a concussion or having bleeding in my brain,* I later thought. So much can happen in one hour.

As I lay on a gym mat on the floor, waiting to be saved by my parents, they barricaded me with chairs all around. I felt like quite the spectacle as I heard my peers whispering, "What happened to her?"

Unbeknownst to me, I had an admirer that had seen the accident who was concerned for me.

Well, thank God someone cares, I thought.

I didn't recognize him but he seemed to know me. As he came rushing into the gym, arms up in the air, he yelled, "I need to know if she's OK! Let me see her!"

Well, I was just lying there, dizzy and embarrassed so I pretended to have amnesia.

"Who are you?" I asked.

LETTERS TO MOM AND DAD

My mom picked me up and took me straight to the hospital where I would be given a series of tests. They sent me home to rest and told my mom to watch for a concussion, although it didn't seem that I had one. The next day, my cousin was having a birthday party and there I was in front of all these kids, with a huge bump on my forehead and two black eyes. As I looked at my swollen forehead, my dreams of becoming a fashion model were shattered. I certainly didn't see my gentlemen friend that day. He must have fallen out of love real fast when he saw my face. From then on, the bump made its way down my face which became distorted over the course of the next few weeks. To this day, I have a bump or an extra layer of skin on my forehead with a little patch of blonde hair reminding me again of why I never went back to any sort of summer camp.

After my family went back to Greece, my father quickly found an apartment and I started a new school again. Mrs. Gilbert, my fifth grade teacher, who resembled my grandmother with her gray hair and glasses, took to me and I was pretty satisfied with her teaching abilities. However, I laid out some ground rules; I was not going to participate in the Pledge of Allegiance every morning as I was not an American citizen, nor did I wish to be. I enjoyed telling people that I was an alien. I had finally found a label to describe how I really felt about myself, so I would stay true to my British roots. I would get up when everyone stood up to the voice on the intercom would start the Pledge of Allegiance and go outside of the classroom and wait for it to be over. Looking back, I believe I had the British superiority complex, I'm sure the Queen would have been proud.

I started to get involved with school activities such as band practice, but according to my father "money didn't grow on trees," so a Steinway was out of the question, and the only instrument left for me to rent for free was the oboe. So I became an oboist.

On our opening night I wore my white Vidal Sassoon pedal pushers which to me were definitely more exciting than playing the oboe. I thought of myself as being fashion conscious and if I was going to play this atrocious instrument, I was going to do it in style. I already felt like an outcast, the alien I knew I was. Stings' "Englishman in New York" rang in my head as I sat in the group, and I secretly wished that I was at least playing the clarinet.

The oboe resembled the clarinet from far away but the clarinet players were positioned in a different area in the seating of the band. There was an instrumental ranking and I definitely was not in the front of the band. Nevertheless, being musically inclined I pushed myself to learn and be the best oboist I could be until its rent was up.

Later, my parents would buy me a flute. It was shiny and beautiful and I felt taller and more important when I played it. But at our school note burning ceremony my nerves got the best of me. I stood there facing all the parents and important people observing this special day. My face was blank as I forgot where I was, who I was, and what I was doing there. I kept stopping in the middle of the song and laughing. My partner just stood there in embarrassment and the whole auditorium just glared at me. It seemed like it took an hour to get through the three minute song. My parents were probably planning their escape early from the ceremony. After much stopping and starting and giggling, I finally pulled it together and started over and played the whole song. At the end of the song, I saw a clear bubble above my partners head, written inside "moron," as she glared at me.

My mom would take me for flute lessons every week against my will. I never liked reading directions and didn't think I needed lessons in anything. I hated going to someone's house to be ordered around. If I wanted to be told what to do I could have just gone home after school and gotten the same treatment.

"There's a list on the refrigerator of your chores, don't forget to walk the dog and clean the pool. Oh yes, and Zoe, tidy up your room, I can't even walk in it, it's so messy!" my mom would say as she was dashing out of the house with her cup of tea in hand to go to work.

"See you on the lift!" she'd yell.

I would complain as she picked me up from school and drove me like she was chauffeuring me around to my flute lessons. REO Speedwagon's "Keep on Loving You" played on the radio and I would think of how I would rather be at home watching *General Hospital*. She would call me ungrateful and threaten to stop the lessons and I would agree in hopes that she would turn the car around but she kept driving. We would always go back every week like clockwork.

LETTERS TO MOM AND DAD

NOGALES

While I was in summer camp I met a Mexican girl named Janna. Our families would eventually hit it off and have barbeques and dinners at each other's houses.

She had a slumber party in her basement. Her mom made us chocolate chip pancakes and we watched Ozzy Osborne videos before we played the game "light as a feather, stiff as a board." We got in a circle with one person in the middle and after chanting "light as a feather, stiff as a board" it was known that the person in the middle would elevate. I can't remember the outcome but we might have rubbed shoulders with the dead that night.

Her family would invite us over for holidays like Thanksgiving and they quickly became like family to us. One time, we went to visit their family in Nogales and watched the Thanksgiving parade. We obviously didn't have that in England. We ate turkey and pumpkin pie and Janna and I played with her cousins. I still wasn't sure what Thanksgiving meant but there were a lot of "gobble gobbles" and food. All I knew was that if it always consisted of this much food, sign me up for next year.

When we all got our Green Cards about a year prior, the first thing we did was drive to Mexico. We were so excited but decided to stay close to the border because we had heard "stories." This was our first family vacation. When we got there we decided that we would like an authentic Mexican lunch and went to the information desk to find out where the best Mexican restaurant was located.

Looking back it sounds a little redundant. But we were on vacation and my father wanted us to experience the best on our first vacation as a family. So we took directions from the information desk and started walking.

When we got to the restaurant, we eagerly waited for our menus anticipating a delicious Mexican meal. When we ordered our food the waiter brought us chips and salsa. As I was digging my chip into the bowl of salsa, I discovered a piece of gum.

"EEEWWWW, look!" I yelled.

My parents were horrified and immediately called on the waiter. The waiter asked what was wrong and we showed him the gum floating around in the salsa.

"No problem!" he said, smiling and put his fingers in the salsa and took the gum out and walked away.

After losing our appetite, we decided to walk around the town and shop. There were children begging, asking for money, and I remember wondering where their parents were. There were bright colors everywhere and shopkeepers inviting us to enter their store. There were all kinds of knick knacks to buy including hats and pottery.

There were huge paper flowers, all different colors that caught my eye and I asked if I could have one.

"Oh no," my mom said, "Those are not good for your allergies."

Oh the good old allergy excuse, I thought.

She had taken me to the allergist in downtown Phoenix where they did a series of scratch tests on my back. Sitting on the table, half naked, being probed, I wondered if this is what it's like to be captured by aliens. Following the scratch test I would find out the many allergies I had and be subjected to getting shots every two weeks for what seemed like years.

My mom would change my sheets and get me a special pillow. I thought I might have to be quarantined the way she was going on about it. I wasn't allowed to have anything that collected dust --which was practically everything. So my beautiful Mexican paper flowers were an impossible dream.

LETTERS TO MOM AND DAD

THE EYES THAT HAD NINE LIVES

Everyone always said I had my Yia Yia's eyes. "Smiling eyes" they said. So you would think that I would treat them like precious commodities. When I was ten I started wearing glasses and realized that having "four eyes" was not going to make me popular. So to add to my big breasts, my lankiness, and crew cut were these bulky glasses sitting on my Roman nose (which my father called "The Concorde").

One night, my friend Jenny was staying the night. It was so hot, especially in our house. The popular item selling in Arizona at the time was a mini fan. Everybody had them. As my friend and I stayed up late dilly dallying, listening to Duran Duran and gushing over John Stamos, we noticed that the wing was broken to my mini fan. Since I prided myself in fixing things, I thought twelve o'clock midnight might be a good time to take this on. So I hunted down some superglue and got to work. Without realizing that the power switch was broken on the fan, I tried to glue the wing back on when suddenly the power turned on and a spec of super glue flew into my eye.

"Ellen, Ellen! Mr. Papadopoulos! Zoe got superglue in her eye!" Jenny yelled bursting into my parents' bedroom.

Waking them up out of a dead sleep, my mom jumped out of bed while my father was swearing in

Greek, "Gamoto!" I was in the bathroom crying rinsing out my eye and looking in the mirror at the spec of superglue stuck in the middle of my iris. Panicking, we all piled into the car and went to the emergency room where they flushed and they flushed and they flushed until they could not flush anymore. The sucker was still in my eye.

So I went home with a patch on my eye looking like a pirate. They told me to come back in two weeks when they would fly out a surgeon from California to cut it off.

As I walked around with this patch on my eye, I could still hear my parents, "What were you doing up that late? Where did you find that glue? What were you thinking? Don't you have any sense, Zoe? You could go blind!"

But when I went back to the doctors they said that by some miracle it was gone. I had dodged a bullet.

At about fifteen I decided to wear contacts. I went to the eye doctor and they showed me how to clean them

"Don't forget to do both steps; you need to rub them and let them soak to clean and then you need to do the second step."

For some reason I would forget the second step, pop them in my eyes and burn my eyeballs. When I went back to the eye doctor with my burnt eyeballs, after making several trips to the emergency room, she scolded me.

"How can you forget the second step? It's not that hard, Zoe."

Then I had to go back a second time. "You're the only one that has a problem with this."

I looked down in humiliation and said, "Sorry, I will try to remember."

What I wanted to say is "Bitch, please. I'm fifteen-years-old. Do you know the kind of pressure I am under? I'll take my business elsewhere."

It was a mistake I would make over and over. Then they came out with one step solution. I wanted to go back and throw my old solution in her face and watch her scream in pain as her eyeballs burned, just like mine had. Later on I would end up scratching my eyes constantly whether from rubbing them too much or by ripping my contacts while wearing them. Finally, I stabbed myself in the eye with some tweezers while working at a cosmetics counter. My poor eyes could write a book themselves on the trauma they have endured.

LETTERS TO MOM AND DAD

STAIRWAY TO HEAVEN

We came back late from our summer vacation in England and when we got off the plane, again I felt like I had stepped into an oven. The skin on my face tightened and a wave of heat came over me as I inhaled hot, dry air. For a second I thought I might be in hell. So I made a mental note of this feeling in case I decided to make any deals with the devil in the future. While driving home, the song "Hot in the City" by Billy Idol was playing on the radio. Instead of yelling "New York!" in the original song they had changed it to "Phoenix!" and that seemed so appropriate in the dead of August.

My father surprised us with a new furnished house to live in and me, a new private school to go to. There was a Jacuzzi in the back patio which was exciting because I had only seen them in rich people's back yards. It was especially exciting to the "peeping Tom" that was about to make an appearance while we were watching television, specifically Michael Jackson's "Thriller." Thank God I only got to see his head pop up over the wall and then he disappeared.

"Khristos! We have a peeping Tom!" my mother said running to my father when he came home from work.

My father, tired from working twelve hours said, "Ah Ellen, just give him a little flash, make the bastard happy."

While we were away, unbeknownst to me, he had enrolled me in a private Christian school. I was a little sad as I never got to say goodbye to all my friends from my previous school, especially the one who I picked up off the ground by the throat when she was teasing me about my British accent. I was sorry that I didn't get to say goodbye to Mrs. Gilbert but she was probably tired of me playing 'eenie meenie minie moe' with true and false questions on her tests anyway. Passing my classes by throwing questions out to the universe was a ritual I would learn later on in life.

When I got to my new school the teachers escorted us into church where I would witness a series of bizarre experiences. For a second, I thought I might be in Jonestown. I saw people with their hands raised, animated, speaking in tongues. At this point church had become a regular chore so I was used to the idea of it, especially if the opposite sex was involved. But I didn't know there was another language that existed. I was used to going to Greek schools wherever we moved but now I had to learn another language? I would later anticipate snakes and dancing around like I saw on *Dateline*. And I definitely avoided any beverages offered to me.

Along with learning a new language I also had to attend rock seminars where they would bring the whole school to the auditorium and sit us down and talk about rock music. We would be lectured on how rock music was the devil's music.

"It is Satan's music, that is how he pulls you in," they proclaimed.

Well, if that's the case, I thought, *Satan and I have become best friends*.

The good news was they played great music such as Queen, The Beatles, and Led Zeppelin. The bad news is that we were all going to hell for listening to it. We would sit in the auditorium while they played music backwards, forwards, and sideways and told us it was Satan's music. Then we would leave and go back to our classes like nothing had happened, in a catatonic state, unaware of what just really took place.

This was a little much for an 11–year-old as I still lived up to my title as the "alien."

"She has a funny accent," I'd hear the kids whisper. I was tall and lanky with big breasts, a buzz cut and buck teeth from sucking my thumb for too long. They called me Zoe Elastic because I was so tall.

If I was green I could be E.T.'s girlfriend, I thought.

My breasts had developed more than the average girl and I started wearing a bra when I was ten. My mom was concerned about my growth spurt and when she took me to the doctor they told her that I was developing fast because of the hormones in the chicken. My hair was cut an inch off of my head because of a bad haircut I got when we were in England. Our family friend, Marge, had convinced a hair dresser to cut my hair like Joan Jett. I thought it looked chic but my mom thought I looked too mature. I would think my maturity came from the C-cup I had acquired (which apparently was the talk of my home town back in England) but she was convinced it was the hair. So she had another hair dresser chop it all off. She tried to convince me that it looked French and sophisticated but we all knew that I looked like a boy with breasts on a stick.

SUPERFREAK

My father was a typical Greek father. He drove me to Greek school every Monday against my will. I'd get into the front seat of his diesel Rabbit, while he hauled ass down Seventh Street in Phoenix. "Super Freak" by Rick James would be blasting from the radio while he chained smoked his Carltons, dancing in his seat. He would drop me off at the Greek Orthodox Church where I sat for three hours learning Greek.

"Alpha, Beta, Gamma, Delta....." I repeated back to the teacher.

I would resentfully turn in my assignments and collect more for the following week, secretly hoping a monsoon might cause the classes to stop. On the plus side, on our way home we would stop for Gyros at his friend's diner. Food always motivated me. We would walk in and the owner's face would light up and he'd start yelling as if he forgot he saw us the week before. They would yell insults at each other, laughing and an occasional Greek swear word like "Malaka" or "Re Pousti" would be thrown about.

Whenever I went into a Greek home or restaurant for dinner, I would be bamboozled into eating more.

"Why haven't you finished your food? Don't you like my cooking? Eat! Eat! You haven't eaten anything! Khristos, what's wrong with Zoe? Is she feeling OK? Is she sick? Maybe she has a fever! Here, eat more, there's plenty of food. Eat! Eat!"

"Zoe, finish your food, there are starving kids in Africa, you know," my father would say.

"You don't know how good you've got it."

The problem is that it was hard to argue with someone who actually lived in Africa. I would always leave stuffed, unable to fasten my pants and vowing never to go back.

Even though my father was overprotective and strict, he always found a way to make me smile usually from the absurdities that came out of his mouth or the jokes he played on people. He worked twelve hours days, under a lot of pressure and I would often call him while he was in a simulator room. He would come home and sit in his Lazy Boy chair and just sit there in deep thought either with his knuckles in his mouth or a cigarette lit.

He was so intensely deep in thought that the only thing that would snap him out of it was food. Sometimes he would help me with my homework but since I liked to cut corners and bypass directions he would just get frustrated with me and send me to my room.

"Did you read this? No! You didn't read it. Now go back to your room, open your book and read the directions," he'd say, "use your loaf!"

I then realized that asking an aerodynamicist for help in geometry was probably a waste of time. To him it was probably the equivalent of making a cup of coffee.

His office was as bad as my room. There were papers all over the place. There were crumpled up papers next to the waste paper basket that had been thrown but missed. His desk was disheveled and it was impossible to find anything on it. My mom and I were told repeatedly to stay away from it. As if it had secret powers. But of course when he lost something, it was because we touched something on his desk.

"I told you not to touch my desk!" he'd 'rant and rave' my mom would say. "Your father's got a bee in his bonnet."

"Apparently he's lost a very important paper" she would say all concerned as if it were the Declaration of Independence.

He would have anything from bills, statements, pay stubs to fake lottery tickets. He had a message pad on his desk with a picture of a naked guy with his head stuck up his ass which said: "Your Problem is Obvious!"

The lottery tickets were for a prank his friend and he would do parked outside a convenient store. They would sit and wait for the idiot that was about to make a phone call at the payphone and watch them pick up the lottery ticket and jump for joy thinking that they had won millions of dollars. Then they would videotape them, laughing while they went to go to claim their so called millions inside the convenient store. But one day after one of his pranks, the tables would be turned as I saw my father flying out the bathroom screaming and swearing because he had accidentally brushed his teeth with Ben Gay.

At this point he had lived in the States for at least nine years and you would think he just moved from a Greek village because I wasn't allowed to date or shave my legs until later in high school. I would sneak out with a bag of clothes and makeup and go to the skating rink. Unfortunately for him, marrying a nice Greek boy was starting to look unreasonable since much of the population in Arizona was Mexican or Native American. So they hoped that by forcing me to go to our next door neighbor's grandson's Bar Mitzvah, a nice Jewish boy would be close enough.

"He's such a nice young man," my mom would say.

"He comes from a good family," my father would mumble.

But if he didn't have tattoos and a foul mouth, I wasn't interested. Those were my standards and I was sticking to them.

I was boy crazy and always managed to find them, whether it be at the skating rink, the local pool, work, or at church. I managed to keep my boyfriend hidden from my father. The pool is where I met my "Secret Lover" -- the song I dedicated to him on the radio in front of the world -- Jason. He was tall and skinny, with blue eyes, and All-American looking. He lived in an apartment a couple miles away from me with his mom. He was cocky and dangerous and I thought that was exciting. He was a smooth talker and kept me on my toes by disappearing for days. He went to a public school which I also thought was really cool, as my class consisted of only 40 students. He would meet me at my local pool regularly and we would go swimming and make out. He would jump over the wall because you needed a key to get in. I liked guys that took risks, you see.

There was never a dull moment, like the day he showed up in a mink coat and sunglasses smoking a cigarette. I guess he thought he was Don Johnson from Miami Vice. It was summer so the mink coat threw me off a bit. I was speechless as I looked at him with his sunglasses on. He flashed his all American smile at me, "What's up babe?" he said.

I would just hold my stomach as the butterflies twirled. On Christmas day, while listening to my Kajagoogoo tape I had just unwrapped, he called me. He asked if I wanted to meet him at the pool for a swim. So I put on my electric blue Body Glove bathing suit and grabbed a towel and my secret concoction of tanning spray which consisted of iodine, baby oil and my mom's British tea. I sprayed my hair with the black hairspray I got in my stocking (which my mom always left me at the end of my bed). I was going for the Goth look. As I waited and waited which was the tradition in our relationship, I finally decided to go for a swim. When he got there he looked at me a little puzzled.

"What's wrong with your face?" he said.

I had no idea what he meant. I went to the bathroom and to my horror, my face was black. That day we skipped the make out session.

WE'RE ON THE ROAD TO NOWHERE

I was never the athletic type. I would rather hang with the Goth kids, dye my hair black and write dark poetry. I smoked clove cigarettes and listened to Alphaville and Sinead O'Connor. I had heard that I was once quite good at basketball and softball but somehow had developed a fear of balls through the years. In summer school, nobody wanted me on their team if the sport had anything to do with balls such as volleyball, bowling and golf. I would see the ball coming and duck. I was always the last to be picked on a team. I knew that I didn't have an athletic bone in me but decided to give it another try. For the sake of love.

I was going to prom with a "jock" from a public school. This was big. I had always wanted to go to public school. Somehow being a student in the only eleventh grade class in the school with forty kids, I felt like all eyes were on me. And they were. Like the time I wore a t-shirt with a peace sign on the front and a parent called the principal to let him know there was a student wearing the sign of the devil at school. It was explained to me that the symbol of the peace sign was an upside down broken cross. I was shocked at the time but what I should have said was "is that what the "church lady" (SNL) told you?"

This boy and I were set up by my parents, who were friends with his parents. He was popular, athletic and good looking. I knew I had to do something drastic to impress him, so I joined the track team. I would wear my red school sweat suit with our logo, which in itself made me feel athletic. I put my fake braid on (because that's what Madonna would do) and some makeup and got ready to run.

Huffing and puffing, trying to keep up with the other runners, I felt inadequate.

Maybe I should quit the cloves, I thought.

Was this really for me? I could hear my mom's encouraging words, "Zoe, don't be hard on yourself. Just give it a go then."

Sure I was tall and lean but maybe it wasn't meant to be put to good use. It was work for me just to do the stretches before we ran. As I lagged behind, after a couple blocks, I envisioned the first track meet.

Don't think about it, I told myself. Think of anything except for the fact that your heart is going to explode and you might cough up a lung.

Suddenly a red Volkswagen Bug pulled up slowly next to me. As I saw the runners way ahead of me, I wondered, *What's going on?*

This handsome young guy rolled down his window and smiled.

"Hi" he said. "How's it going? Do you need a ride?"

Don't talk to strangers, I could hear my mom's words echoing in the back of my head."

"Sure," I said, and got in.

We drove around for a while and went to the mall. Then he brought me back to school. Nobody said anything, not even the teacher. The next day I quit the track team.

Since my parents knew the parents of my prom date, I was allowed to stay out as late as I wanted. By now I realized that it just wasn't in me. I was not meant to be a jock's girlfriend; however, I still had to go through with the date. My mom had bought me a beautiful Gunne Sax dress that was fit for a princess. He took me to the Hyatt Regency for dinner and it was a fairy tale evening. But I wanted danger and excitement. I envisioned matching tattoos and Vegas. When my mom sent the family back home in England pictures of us all dressed up, they all thought I had gotten married. I guess they didn't have such a thing there.

LETTERS TO MOM AND DAD

PRETTY IN PINK

I met my first official boyfriend, Logan, in summer school. He was tall, dark, and handsome, just like my father. The big brown eyes and dark brown hair that would swing into his face, Bieber-style, caught my attention. The flashy smile with the flashy clothes and the flashy car was intriguing. I met him in a P.E. class where he showed me his bowling skills and took me for a ride in his red BMW. Apparently, he didn't show up for the first class because he had a hangover. He had me at "hangover."

I had heard people talk about him at church. He had parties at his house where helicopters circled above, and the police were called regularly. Everybody talked about the parties and how wild they were. He was famous and dangerous. He was like the James Bond of the rich high schools. I decided that I needed a bit of excitement in my life and he would be my supplier.

School started and the homecoming dance was coming up. Since he was my boyfriend, he was going to go with yours truly. But he decided to have one of these famous parties the night of our homecoming dance without mentioning it to me, his supposed girlfriend. I was going to a private Christian high school and they didn't have proms, so this dance was a big deal. With only forty spoiled, sheltered students in my class, there was sure to be a lot of drugs, alcohol, and wild, crazy sex (which I hadn't had yet, even at 17). I was what the other kids called "a prude" but I was saving myself because I was not a fan of hot weather and knew what hell felt like. But this dance was a priority.

Well I was completely taken back when Logan was a no show! I was furious! I called him and asked him where he was. He said he had plans.

What could be more important than coming with me to my homecoming dance?

"A party," he said.

I told him it was over between us and hung up devastated. But I stayed. Alone. I was not going to let it ruin my night.

The following year I vowed to win him back, as he was a great catch, you see. What had I done? Why didn't he want me? I had to know! I had to get him back! He was everything! He was the talk of the high school district. The red BMW. The style and charisma. The parties. The police. And the Ralph Lauren attire lured me in once again.

So I showed up on his doorstep on graduation night and to my surprise, he was very receptive. He flashed that All-American smile and I beamed as I sunk into his broad shoulders. It was going to happen! I was going to win him back! I was bronzed (thanks to my mom's British tea), makeup perfect, hair done and looking good so it was the perfect opportunity to just stop by, one year later. Sporting a red nose with my bi-leveled, feathered hairdo and 80's style short pink puffy dress, I told him I might stop by later, if he was lucky. Which I did, but I knew I needed to leave the boy hanging. Drunk and giddy, at around midnight, the whole scene was dreamy, and I was in love. We were back on again! B52's "Summer of Love" rang in my head as I skipped back to my car and dreamed of our future. Then I drove to my "friend" Brian's house. I had to keep my options open.

Little did I know that my crazy Greek father was having Logan followed by his friend who was a police officer. Unfortunately, my rich unemployed boyfriend neglected to tell me that he was "up to no good," as my mom would say. Being a good Christian girl I was mortified. But I was in way too deep as we had taken our portraits together to make it official and I was in love. It was serious. We had pet names for each other and I was getting close to his family.

One day, he came over and we were kissing on my bed, listening to the Psychedelic Furs. That day, I decided to live on the edge, as I was told never to have boys in the house when no one was home. Suddenly I heard my father come in to the house. The dog was barking and I panicked. I pushed Logan into my closet and told him to be quiet. I locked the door and waited, frozen. My father started banging on the door!

"Zoe! Open the door! Open the door! What's going on?!"

I opened the door and tried to act calm.

My father looked around, wide eyed with his crazy, wiry, gray hair and yelled in his Greek accent, "where eez he?"

"What are you talking about?" I said, pretending to be clueless and obviously unaware that Logan's red BMW was parked outside our house.

"I know heez here!" my father yelled.

He looked around then opened the closet and there he was!

"Get out!" my father screamed. "Whoos thu fuck you think you are? You get out right now! You weel neva see my daughter again, do you hear me?!"

I started crying. "You don't understand," I cried, "nothing happened! It's the truth!"

"Oh, I understand!" my father yelled, pointing his finger in my face like he was Jack Nicholson in "A Few Good Men."

"You can't handle the truth!" echoed in my head.

"You've brought shame on this family! Do you hear me Zoe? Shame!"

It was all a little dramatic, I thought.

My father was always dramatic. Our house was loud and animated, like we were in a movie theater. You just needed to bring the popcorn. We were always yelling from room to room. I don't know if it was out of laziness or if the Greek blood just automatically made you louder. I eventually got my own black Swatch phone so I could call my mom in the kitchen to see what was for dinner, rather than hear her yelling, "Zoeeeeee! Dinner's ready!"

But there was always something going on with my father, whether he couldn't find his keys, or lost his hat, or lost his mail, it was like living in an action movie.

My poor mother would run around the house frantically looking for his stuff while she asked a series of questions as if she was interviewing a witness.

"When was the last time you saw it? Where were you the last time you had it? Do you remember who you were with the last time you had it? Let's retrace your steps, Khristos," she'd say, trying to comfort him.

So my boyfriend left in a hurry as expected. Thank God it was time for me to go to work, so I could get out of the chaos and start bagging groceries for eight hours. That would help me clear my head. Heavy cans on the bottom. Bread and chips on the top. Frozen stuff in a separate bag. Meat separate.

"Would you like help to your car?" I'd ask praying to be turned down. I was a little fragile going to work as I had smoked a joint and was little shaken up from the drama. It had all been a little much for a Monday.

Wow, what a buzz kill this was, I thought.

So I went to work in my red Guess jeans that cost me my weekly paycheck and pondered on what I would do without my "honey bunny." I clearly was going to die. He was everything to me. We were in love. We had big plans. He called me "honey bunny." How could this be happening? What would I do without him?

The next day, my father had obviously reevaluated the situation and came to me to discuss it further. He said to tell my boyfriend that if he wanted to see me again, he would have to meet him at the local Carl's Jr. to discuss it. To my surprise Logan agreed. So we all met at Carl's Jr. After answering a few simple questions, over some burgers and fries, such as, "who pays for your car and why don't you work?" it was on again. I don't know what he said to my father but we were back on! Of course, I always felt like we were being followed. But it was thrilling. Always looking over your shoulder. It was like we were unstoppable. He was my James Bond. We were like Bonnie and Clyde, Romeo and Juliet. No one was going to keep us apart. Nobody.

RIDERS ON THE STORM

I was learning how to drive and looking forward to getting a car. Wheels meant wings for me. I couldn't wait. I drove my dad's diesel Mercedes to church and it was like driving a tank. He had also just purchased a Range Rover for my mother. I tried to drive it but one day cut a corner with my father in the car and almost flipped it. My father grabbed the hand break and starting swearing and the next thing I knew I was in the passenger's side.

The Mercedes was his pride and joy and would rarely leave the garage. It had a cover on it and an alarm with a man's voice that told you to back off if you got within a couple inches of it. When he did take it out you could hear him coming home down the street as he had a stereo system installed with woofers.

Charlie, our dog, would run straight to the door. As the garage door opened, I could hear Erasure blasting, "Come to me, cover me, hold me, together we'll break these chains of love" as my dad was dancing in his seat, waving his hands all over the place. When his stereo was on, he didn't have a care in the world.

All my friends loved my dad and thought he was so hip. The loud music I could tolerate. But I regretted the day he purchased M.C. Hammer pants. I watched him in horror dancing around the house with his headphones on while wearing these ridiculous colorful pants. He was like a kid trapped in a man's body. My friends always left my house laughing. They knew there was always a show at the Papadopoulos' house and tickets were free.

But his mood would change when he drove the Range Rover. It ended up being a lemon and was a constant source of drama. It would go back and forth to the dealership numerous times.

"I want to speak to your supervisor!" I'd hear my dad yelling.

"I'm cursed Ellen! I'm cursed!" he'd say to my mom.

Finally, my dad purchased a sun visor for the car with the words, "Looking to buy a Range Rover? Ask me about my nightmare!" He wasn't giving up.

"These people need to understand that they can't get away with this!" he'd say waving his hands, animated and ready for fight. "They are not going to win!" And they didn't.

Anyway, after much hinting, he bought me a car called the Plymouth Sapporo. "Isn't that a Japanese beer?" I would become accustomed to hearing. I had only ever seen them as police cars in Greece but apparently, according to him, they were quite fast. "Racing cars," he said. I sat in that car for hours listening to the stereo visualizing driving my car everywhere. I finally had wings and oddly enough, the car named after a Japanese beer was what gave me them. I felt liberated.

When I got to school I told everyone I got a car and all the popular girls wanted to see it. So it wasn't a Honda Accord or a BMW. It was my car. They rushed out to look, a little confused, as they looked at the purple tinted windows. So what if I didn't have an expensive car? My father believed in "valuing things." "You have to work for money, it doesn't just grow on trees," he'd say.

He knew what he was doing because in the end, the Plymouth Sapporo's life would be short lived.

Just like my father, I loved loud music and the one thing the Plymouth had was a great stereo system. My father was always checking the car for me to see if it was running correctly but after numerous times of starting the car and almost having a heart attack with the music blasting, he'd had enough. He decided to pull the fuse out. I was furious! He of all people should understand how much I loved my music! So I did a little research and went to the auto parts store where they sold me another fuse. I quickly learned about my fuse box as well as checking my oil, which my father showed me how to do.

About a year later, Logan, his sister, Annie and I decided to go out drinking at a local Mexican restaurant that was also known for their happy hour. We all piled into the Sapporo. We never went for the fine Mexican food or even the Margaritas. We went because we could get in. Period. End of story. We would put quarters in the jukebox and listen to The Doors and dance and pretended that we were children of the 60's wearing our patchouli oil and hemp bracelets.

We were driving home and suddenly someone pulled out into the road backwards. I slammed on the brakes but it was too late. We crashed right in the side of his car. I jumped out, anticipating the major damage we had just done, but to my surprise the driver of the other car took off. The front of my car looked like a crushed Coke can.

Now what was I going to do?

We drove back to Logan's house where I just freaked out. My car was totaled. My dad was going to kill me! Annie, the concerned friend that she was, decided that she needed cigarettes which apparently were priority over my accident and asked to borrow my car. Against my better judgment, I let her go.

What's the worst that could happen? I already totaled the front of the car.

After she came back, I tried to drive home, the car was steering to the left but I kept going. When I got home I would see that I had a flat tire. Too frazzled and scared to wake up my parents, I wrote a note to my dad and posted it on the refrigerator, "Dad, got into an accident. We will talk in the morning."

"What duh fuck happened to the car?" I heard my dad yelling as I came to with my head spinning.

My father plowed into my bedroom, bright eyed and bushy tailed (my mom would say).

"Yeah, I got into an accident," I said, trying to shrug it off.

"What happened? Why didn't you call the police? Do you know you have grass in your engine?"

"No, I didn't call the police."

"Why? Why? I know why! You were drinking!!!" his finger pointing in my face.

What would possibly make you think that? I thought. *Could it be the smell of alcohol seeping through my skin? Or the beer bottles on the floor in the front seat of the car. I wasn't drinking!* I convinced myself. *And how could there be grass in my engine? I hit a car, not a park!* I was perplexed.

I had been drinking but I remembered the accident. It was a hit and run! I hit him and he ran! I jumped out of the car to look at the damage and the driver of the other car took off, screeching away. I wasn't surprised as it was in a terrible neighborhood called Sunnyslope. It was so run down we nicknamed it Slummy Slope. There were shady people walking around but as you drove up the mountain, the houses grew more attractive.

A couple years later I would discover that when Annie drove my car, she plowed into someone's front yard and hit their mailbox.

"I really thought it was a rock," she would explain as if that would have made all the difference.

That explained the grass in the engine and the oil pan being dented.

"You'll never be able to get an oil change again!" my father yelled, shaking his head full of disappointment.

Eventually, I received a notice on my car parked outside our house saying it was an eyesore and that they were going to tow it. So, we parked it at my father's friend's house. They both tried to figure out a plan on what to do with the old Plymouth Sapporo. My father spent three days in his friend's bed after trying to fix the bumper. He threw out his back and he probably laid there wondering why he even bothered. Finally they managed to sell it for $250 even though he asked for $300.

"I felt embarrassed when the buyer took it for a test drive and came back walking," he said.

Apparently, the front tire blew up and the engine overheated and they spent five hours trying to fix it. They wanted to pay $200 but settled for $250. Turning the radio up whenever I heard something that didn't sound right with the car wasn't a good idea after all.

ONE FLEW OVER THE CUCKOO'S NEST

As I was running out of my house, he approached me at the walkway. Pastor Jon, our church minister had been summoned to the Papadopoulos household. My parents were concerned about my irrational behavior. I was acting hostile to say the least. I had recently broken up with Logan and made a couple of empty threats such as "I want to kill myself" which didn't go over too well with my parents. I thought it would get someone's attention. And it did. Bent over with arms outstretched like he was blocking a football player, he pleaded, "It's okay Zoe, it's okay."

It felt like he was mediating a hostage situation. With my keys in my hand, ready for escape, Pastor Jon was about to tackle me down to the ground. As I tried to get around him to reach my car, a police car pulled up. Before I knew it I was in a squad car.

Wow, I thought. *This is cool. I'm actually in a police car.*

Who knew I could be so dangerous? If only they could have handcuffed me, I could really brag to my friends. I wondered if the neighbors were watching.

Maybe I'll get a mug shot, I secretly hoped.

I woke up in a locked room.

Do hotels usually lock you in their rooms?   I wondered as I came to.

Feeling pleasantly surprised that I had been sedated, I wandered around to look at the amenities. All my belongings were gone and I needed a cigarette. I discovered a lighter attached to the wall. It was like a mini stove top burner on the wall. People were walking around like zombies. I wandered into a room with a TV on and sat on the couch. As my zombie eyes glared at the TV, I noticed that the movie *Helter Skelter* was on.

Great, I'm a loony watching loonies in a loony bin! This is bound to be an interesting experience, I thought.

The staff showed me to my suite where I would spend my vacation for six weeks. I didn't have a roommate. I got the feeling that summers were slow, so I could do whatever I wanted. I just needed to attend meetings, eat on schedule, and show up for my drugs which would be good practice for my future bartending days. As I looked up at the "12 Steps" on the wall I contemplated what I was powerless over.

There was a colorful bunch of "personalities" in my group ranging from ages 35-55. They all told me how lucky I was to get a head start on my mental health as I was so young at twenty years of age. Janice was a sweet mother of two, married to a pastor, who had tried to kill herself numerous times. She had scars from cutting herself all over her body, from head to toe. Jack, the truck driver found out he was manic depressive when his wife left him with their two children. He was devastated. She thought he was cheating on her because he was out at night when he couldn't go to sleep.

Then there was Jeffrey. He was still stuck in the 80's with his bi-level haircut and thick mustache.

All he needed was a leather ensemble and he could be Freddie Mercury, I thought to myself.

He had electrodes hooked up to his head. They couldn't figure out what was wrong with him. He just walked around looking like a mobile fuse box not a care in the world. Julia was a thin, frail woman whose fingers and toes were curled up so tight that it became a permanent condition. Apparently it was because she hated her mother. Looking like a bag of bones, her mouth was tense and she held her head down all the time. As I observed her, I could see what sadness looked like on the outside.

Then of course, what good is a psychiatric ward without a sex addict.

What's so bad about that? I thought.

I had aspirations of being a prostitute when I was a young girl. I had heard about this activity called sex, which was supposed to be a lot of fun. Everybody wanted to do it. It was supposed to feel really good. My parents had instilled in me values in which they always told me that working hard would lead to success and money so when I heard about a job where you could have sex and get paid, I was in. Sign me up!

We sat in meetings, day after day and we talked about our "feelings." There were punching bags in a room for role playing. As I looked up at the wall that had the twelve steps, I realized that I was definitely not an alcoholic but maybe I was one of these codependent people they talked about. Yes, that's it, I decided. My name is Zoe and I'm co-dependent. Although I was the youngest in the group I suddenly felt like I finally belonged. I liked it there. I didn't want to leave and go back to working at Broadway Southwest as a contingent. What would I do when I got out? Couldn't I stay here forever? Eventually, I would be discharged and sent to face the real world again.

"Now you need to make sure you keep taking this medication," the psychiatrist said during my out-patient visit. And make sure you don't drink." he said firmly.

Yes, I will take my medication. Drink? Of course I need a drink! It was time to celebrate my departure from the loony bin so my friends and I went out to Tempe where a poor under-aged girl fresh out of a mental institute would easily blend in. I went straight to the bars. I listened to him like I listened to my father about getting a tattoo. I wanted a psychedelic flower on my foot but I knew my father would never approve. So when I came home I proudly showed him my foot hoping he would change his mind when he saw the work of art on my foot. But he just mumbled, "If you want to ruin your life, go ahead."

The Greeks were always exaggerating. Everything was such a big deal. It was a flower. But you would think I had gotten a swastika on my forehead.

LETTERS TO MOM AND DAD

YIA YIA

My father and I decided to go to Greece to see my grandmother, as she was sick. While on the plane, a handsome Italian man approached me about modeling. I was clearly flattered. I had my leather biker jacket on with my painted red lips as I conveniently struck a pose while putting away my luggage. I was considered tall and quite attractive after I got my braces off, so it wasn't a farfetched idea. My dad on the other hand was skeptical. We had never heard of him even though he said he was a fashion designer. He said that he knew people in New York that could help me have a modeling career. He was charming and distinguished, young and attractive, and he spoke with an Italian accent. He opened his sports jacket and sure enough, his name was inside of his jacket. Of course, he had to prove himself to my father, and although it was farfetched that he had OCD and felt the need to label all his jackets with his name on them, he later sent pages and pages of magazine articles that were written about him. Forbes couldn't lie, and I was off to New York.

I had always dreamed of being a model so I begged my dad to agree to let me go. My father allowed me to go with my mom and we hit the Big Apple. The agency put us up in a beautiful penthouse across from Central Park. I met with them; they gave me a t-shirt, and sent me on castings and test-shoots all over the city.

For a week, my mom and I walked the streets of New York endlessly, jumping from train to train with our maps in hand, like tourists. I did some test- shoots and then went back to the agency to hear what they had to say. "You look too much like this up and coming model Greta (who looked exactly like Linda Evangelista) so there isn't a market for you right now."

OK, I can't work because I look like an upcoming model that looks like a supermodel.

Hmmmmm (my pretty brain went into overdrive). *So what did they say to her when they realized that she looked like an upcoming model?* I thought.

Just like every model aspires to hear, they told me to go back to Arizona, go to the gym and come back when I was ready. At 122 pounds, and 5'8 ½", I was very disappointed to say the least.

I went back to Arizona and signed with an agency.

At least they believed in me, I thought.

I was insecure and hadn't been taught how to move in front of the camera yet. My heart would race when going to see photographers.

What do I do? How do I move? Do I smile and show my huge teeth? Am I skinny enough? Pretty enough?

I was scared as I watched the models prance in and out of the agency. We all looked each other up and down. The photographers would flip through the books, sometimes barely looking at the pictures. And I would leave feeling more and more inadequate. But somehow I knew the process would make me stronger. One photographer took an interest in me right away and we started doing some test shooting. His wife was a makeup artist and they had their studios in their house in Phoenix. They took me under their wing. They had their "ideas" and believed in me. The pictures were creative and beautiful and I started to get my confidence back. I changed my diet as I realized the expectations and started counting fat grams. I also joined the gym. However, my idea of a warm-up was standing in the tanning booth for 15 minutes. I was not very motivated. Diet pills and laxatives would later become my friends although not a good partner with marijuana as I had a sweet tooth.

I went back to Greece to say a final farewell to my Yia Yia. We stayed in the house that my father grew up in, in a town called Glyfada, where I also spent many summers with my Yia Yia. When I got there, she was lying in bed dying. She was so frail and skinny unlike the last time I saw her. She had been full of life, laughing and chain smoking on the bed playing cards with her friend, Eliki. She was a tall, large woman but always dressed very classy and had beautiful clothes, shoes and handbags. Now she was all bones with a turban wrapped around her head to disguise her baldness. Her face was sunken in and her body looked like matchsticks floating around under the sheets.

I walked into the room and saw my father sitting next to her as she laid there dying. He was talking to her and when he saw me he said to her, "Look Mama, Zoe is here!" with great enthusiasm in his voice.

She could barely hold her head up to look at me smiling at her. She looked empty and hollow. She didn't know who I was. She looked lost and confused. The cancer had spread to her brain and she was losing her memory, and going in and out of consciousness. My Yia Yia was dying. I pulled out a silver bracelet with heart links that I had bought her and put it in her bony hands. It clung to her fingers like it was the last time it would be held. She looked at me and her eyes lit up as if she suddenly remembered me.

People always said I had her eyes. They were piercing and telling. Looking into her eyes was like looking into mine. You could always tell what she was feeling through her eyes, when she was angry and especially when she was happy. I was told that I smiled through my eyes.

Maybe that's why I was named after her, I thought.

Tears welled up in her eyes as she looked at me remembering me for a split second and smiled. Then she drifted again.

My cousins and I went out to some local bars to have a few drinks. We stayed out for a few hours and when we came home she was gone. Her bed was empty and the house was quiet. I cried myself to sleep. I felt so guilty for not being there when she passed. In the middle of the night, I felt a hand grab my arm and I jolted awake. I was stunned. I felt a presence but there was no one there.

Is that you, Yia Yia?

My heart was racing. Later I would find out that the neighbors said they saw a silhouette of her walking on the balcony outside my room.

A couple weeks later, I would come back to an empty house and when I walked into her room, all her pills were pulled out of the closet. They were spread all over the floor and the bed. Her room was upside down. I asked my cousins and my aunt if they had done it and they said no. They hadn't been home all day.

Could she be trying to send a message? I thought.

Maybe it was her way of letting us know she didn't appreciate us smoking. We would sit out on the marble balcony that we had played on as children and smoke cigarette after cigarette laughing and chatting away. I could see her looking down on us, shaking her head in disappointment as we were following in her footsteps.

It seemed like all of Athens came to her funeral. Everybody knew her. As a child, she would take me out to the grocery store and people would stop her on the streets. They would converse and then I would ask, "Yia Yia, who was that?"

"I don't know," she laughed.

My grandfather knew so many people and had been very wealthy at one time. He was an elephant hunter in Africa, owned a plantation, and helped build a hospital. But they moved back to Greece after my father's brother died of malaria. He loved to gamble and would have the military sit outside his house while he entertained the generals. My grandmother would give him a hard time about his gambling and threaten to leave. They would fight and he would storm out. He would disappear and come home later with flowers and all would be forgiven. Sadly, he had a heart attack and died when I was about two.

I remember him leaving one day, waving goodbye, smiling as he went down the steps out the kitchen door (where the "evil eye" hung above) but he never returned. She told me later that the clock in the living room stopped on the hour of the day he died.

The church was packed as people paid their respects. I had only ever been to two other funerals but the amount of people at hers was overwhelming. The last time I was in a Greek Orthodox Church in Greece was when we came to live with my grandmother when I was seven. She wanted me to go to Greek school so I had to be baptized. Since we didn't know too many people, her tenants living upstairs volunteered to be my

Godparents. It was unusual for someone to be baptized at my age and I was unsure of what I was getting myself into.

My Godmother made me a beautiful white dress with a matching head band. As I reluctantly made my way to the church, the smell of incense crowded the air and I saw a group of people that I barely knew, standing there watching. I wondered what was about to take place. Before I knew it, there was a conversation between the priest and my grandmother and my clothes were removed.

What's going on? I panicked.

There I was standing in my Wonder Woman underwear as the priest immersed me into the water. When everything was said and done (and there was a lot to be said and done including olive oil being placed on me), I walked away confused and smelling like a Greek salad. Everyone else left with candy almonds in beautiful white sachets.

LETTERS TO MOM AND DAD

FREEDOM

I walked the streets of Athens, unaware of the turn of events to come. Finally, I walked into an agency and a handsome man with chiseled cheek bones and perfectly placed hair looked at me over some paperwork and asked me if he could help. My heart skipped a beat. The George Michael look-a-like flashed his perfect smile and I stumbled over my words, shy and embarrassed. I stepped forward and told him I was interested in signing with an agency in Greece. He looked at my book and this charming, handsome man, drank me in with his eyes. On the wall there were pictures of him with supermodels such as Christy Turlington. I was impressed and star struck.

Stavros, my future agent, conveniently lived in my hometown. It was all too good to be true and things seemed to fall right into place. He said that if I signed with him, he would forward me enough money to come back from America and pay for living accommodations. He told me that I had a job waiting for me. My father talked to him on the telephone and the two Greeks discussed my modeling career. My father, who had never embraced my modeling career in the past, agreed to let me come back alone and work. I was ecstatic.

Freedom! I thought.

Yanni's Pension in Athens was right by the Acropolis. The area was called Koukaki. The streets were narrow and curvy with alleyways down the sides, making it easy for one to get lost. When you walked in, there was the "front desk" where there may or may not be someone to help you depending on your luck. Behind the desk were composite cards with models and actors on them pinned to the wall.

Would I give him my composite card? I wondered.

A little boy flew by me giggling, and behind him was a woman scolding him, I assumed his mother. I climbed the tiny, winding stairs and unpacked my suitcase which mainly consisted of caramel flavored rice cakes. I had learned early on that rice cakes were a models best friend and I couldn't find them in Greece. My room was small but had a balcony so I could open the windows and breathe the toxic Athenian air which would end up causing my constant colds. There were three beds and a side table in between. The hotel was noisy with self-absorbed, chattering models and I was excited for this new venture. I unpacked my suitcase and lay down on the tiny bed and drifted away.

A few days later, I had a German roommate named Anke. We would sit up for hours at night while she read my tarot cards and told me my future which was conveniently always bright. I hung on to her every word as if she were the Dali Lama. We would wake up, have a frappe (Greek iced coffee) and a cigarette, then call the agency for them to give us a list of castings to go to. She didn't take modeling seriously and would often blow off the castings. She also didn't have the model look and wasn't really motivated. I remember wondering why she was even there. I soon discovered that she had a cute American boyfriend. Now I understood. He was an unlucky surfer who was discovered by Guess on the beach in California. He had only been in Greece for one week, was at the peak of his modeling career finishing up a Guess campaign, when he got hit by a car, broke his leg, and was confined to his room in a basement across the street from the hotel. Anke would soon turn his luck around as she paid many visits to him and took care of his every need. She would later introduce me to his roommate, Joe.

I started to find my way around Athens. Kolonaki was fast paced. There were lots of cafés with people drinking their frappés, smoking their cigarettes, and chatting for hours. Since it was during the work week, I wondered if they had jobs. There was a kiosk in every corner where you could buy anything, from a phone card to a magazine or a chocolate croissant. Every time I stopped at a corner or traffic light I found myself needing something to eat or drink.

The shops were filled with luxurious clothing in the windows and the mannequins would lure me in. The sales people were often outside either smoking or trying to get some air. Either way, it would be toxic. I loved to pass by the Body Shop and smell the familiar smells that reminded me of

America. The smell of the soaps would drag me in. Then, when I moved back to America, I would love to go into the Body Shop to remember my days in Athens. I would pick up the soaps and breathe in the memories.

02/02/1993

Dear Mom and Dad,

Well, I live in a hotel, if that's what you want to call it. It's more like a dorm. I live in a room with three beds about as big as my room (a little bigger). It has a closet and a balcony, a tiny dressing table and a bathroom. The shower has no door so you can imagine the mess afterwards. But there's a lot of hot water even though Yanni said he had to cut it down because of the new law. He and dad would get along great since he also doesn't believe in heating either. Anyway, it costs 3,500 drachmas ($14) to do two loads of washing – that's the cheapest I've found. The hotel is right next to the acropolis in Koukaki. There are lots of markets to get things also. We also have a tiny refrigerator under our microscopic dressing table. And there's a hole that everyone refers to as the kitchen here. You can cook whatever. Lately my roommate and I have been making macaroni.

I'm so glad you bought me deodorant and contact lenses stuff and all that stuff because there is no way I could buy it. I ran out of money but *the agency should advance me $100 a week. The first week I was here I spent a hundred dollars on taxis. But now I go to castings with other girls and it works out cheaper. And I'm trying to learn the bus system. The agency gave us a map in English which is useful. Without it I would be lost. I wish I had my tennis shoes because I have blisters on my feet from walking so much. Every day I go to about five castings. So far I have had two catalog jobs and a bank commercial in Cyprus.*

Some of the models go out every night of the week (like my roommate) but I just go on the weekend. And when we go out we all go out together (usually five to ten models) and we don't pay to get in and if there's a line we cut in front and they let us go right in. There is a reserved section for all of us and of course we don't pay for our drinks. It's nice to be treated like kings and queens. Everyone stares like they've never seen a beautiful person before in their life. I feel so powerful now. When I go to castings I don't feel intimidated by the clients because most of the time they're so disorganized they don't know what the hell they're doing. I did lose a job (possible job) because I refused to drink the Greek milk. I couldn't. I would gag.

My roommate is German. She's twenty one and bought property with her boyfriend and built seven apartments. She lives off that money. She's been here for a month and hasn't worked. But she also blows off some of her castings. She's crazy but really fun. She's also a psychic and has read my mind. Yes I know- be careful. You don't know her very well, she could be dangerous. She could be involved with the devil....

I don't even need you here anymore with me to nag at me because it just echoes in the back of my head whenever something even interesting pops up in my life. Oh by the way – I heard Stavros is bisexual, but prefers men- so you have nothing to worry about.

I have visited Auntie Eleni twice since I've been here a week. She buys me big tins of nuts and gives me fruit. God knows I stuff my face there because I can't afford to eat like that here. They even tell me that I'm eating like a pig but I can't help it.

Anyway- I have to go to bed it's ten o'clock. Tomorrow's Monday. Pretty scary huh? When I go to bed my roommate is getting ready to go to the clubs. Everyone parties so much here.

Last night I locked myself out of the hotel and it was a nightmare. I couldn't pay the taxi driver because I didn't have my wallet. But he was nice about it. I even managed to get him to buy me some souvlaki- he felt sorry for me because I was locked out and it was so cold. Then I was so frustrated. I was crying because Yanni doesn't wake up until eight am and it was six thirty am. By noon the whole hotel knew about it. Everybody kept saying, "Oh, you're the one who got locked out of your room."

Yanni is sort of strict. He doesn't like you to wear a bathing suit on the roof and whenever my roommate comes home from her boyfriend's apartment the next morning he always looks at her disapprovingly like he's her father. He also has my passport. I guess everybody in the hotel has to give it to him and he locks them up. He says he has to because they check him out to see if the models are staying longer than they should. They get a three month holiday visa.

Anyway, time to go to bedibyes,

Love Zoe

Anke and I settled in to our little place quite nicely. We would stay up late and talk about our lives back home and the people that we left behind. We would gossip about the other models, what castings we went to, and who we thought got the job.

Being on a budget, I would cook spaghetti for us almost every night since it was the cheapest thing to buy. We would end up stealing the plates and forks from the stove area because we could never find any. In the daytime I lived off of coffee and cigarettes.

Anke wasn't too serious about castings. She seemed more interested in going out. But I was serious and tried to make all of them. I shared taxis with other models and tried to take the bus as I was getting tired of walking everywhere. I took pride in being a working model, even though I was always running out of money. I still felt independent.

02/25/1993

Hello Mom and Dad

Well I was bored sitting in my room alone tonight so I thought I'd write you a letter. My roommate is working. We get along really well. We are a lot alike - very messy. We also have plates and forks in our room which looks bad. We only clean them if we need to use them. We stole them from the kitchen because otherwise the others take them to use and don't return them soon enough. I just did my washing today. It cost me fifteen dollars. I never thought I'd appreciate doing my own laundry at home but it would be a lot cheaper. Well, I'm working tomorrow which is good because I was running out of money. I received a printout of all my earnings this month and expenses. So far I've made $2,200 but I've spent all of it almost every week. I ask for about $100-$150 a week for living expenses. Then for one week rent is about $75. For the two thousand dollars I made in one month I only worked five days (including commercial).

LETTERS TO MOM AND DAD

I might move out of Yanni's in a couple weeks. He's always complaining about everything. The music is too loud, we use too much hot water, we can't have visitors (mainly boys) in our room and we can't use the stove after 11:00 and sometimes we don't get our telephone messages until two days later. Shit, if I wanted all that I might as well come back home! Haha.

I have to get my shoes fixed also. I wore the whole heel off of the brown boots you bought me. And also with my black boots. I walk a lot. But now if I have time I take the bus. Sometimes I even take it for free. It's my way of getting back at the taxi drivers for screwing me with money so much or refusing me because they don't know the address. I save a lot of money taking the bus or going to castings with two or three other girls. It's hard not to be able to buy clothes and stuff I would buy in Phoenix. You know that when you take the soap and shampoo from hotels, salt and toilet paper from restaurants and steal cigarettes from other models that you're pretty desperate. But I have enough to eat and get around.

Anyway I must go- I have to make my appearance at a club tonight because it's a special night and you never know the important people you might meet.

Love Zoe

LETTERS TO MOM AND DAD

MODELO

When I had some money saved, I purchased a pair of lace up boots. It was exciting to finally have some money. I was starting to look like a working model. I would stroll into my agency and discuss jobs and pick up checks. The agency would set up dinners for us and nights out in night clubs. I met lots of male models but was spending a lot of time with Anke and her boyfriend who introduced me to his roommate, also from California. He wasn't that good looking, but was very photogenic. He was cocky and full of himself and that always lured me in. I would tease him for listening to Frank Sinatra and it never amounted to anything except bickering. I didn't really find him that attractive; he annoyed me and antagonized me, but somehow I found myself attracted to him. My low standards had resurfaced.

Anke and I would sit in the basement drinking beer while the boys popped painkillers. I would call this the typical model's date as they were so cheap I'm surprised they didn't send us out to buy the beer. One night he told me his "friend" Carlos Salvador was in town. He was a famous American actor filming a movie there. He was known for his good looks and bad boy image. I just laughed at him.

If he knew Carlos Salvador why would he be living in a basement in Athens? I thought.

That night I went out and sure enough ran into his "friend" drinking shots of whiskey with women all around him.

That would have been a better date at least, I thought.

During the week, a gaggle of models would pile into a taxi and we'd share the fare to the castings. We would get to our locations and we would all be trying to figure out the currency as the taxi drivers patiently waited. When we needed to hail a taxi, the taxi drivers had a system. If they nodded their head up, it meant "Where are you going?" If they nodded their head up and raised their eyebrows it meant "no" and if they nodded their head to the left, it meant "get in." I would be the leader of the gaggle as I understood this code quite well. I would stand on the curb exchanging glances and nods with taxi drivers and the models would wait for me to signal. "Get in! Hurry up!" I'd yell. There was no sense of urgency with them as they didn't realize that the Greeks were pretty impatient and would have no problem moving on to the next unsuspecting customer, especially if they didn't recognize the address. When we got in, I would mention that I was Greek so that they wouldn't take us on a tour of Athens while their meter was running before taking us to our destination.

On the weekends, we would go to the Acropolis, walk around and buy beads at the bead shop or go to the flea market. People would stare at us on the streets and you could hear them whisper "modelo."

When I was alone it was uncomfortable, but when I was in a group I felt like a rock star. On Sundays, there was a farmers market on the street below my room and I would wake up to the hustle and bustle of the Greeks selling produce. It was far louder than the American farmers market. I would stand on the balcony and watch the chaos going on and wonder if there was a war going on below us.

Yanni took a liking to me as I had a Greek last name. He was very strict with the models. We weren't allowed to have overnight guests, but he would make an exception with my Greek boyfriend, Costas. The Greeks were always loyal to each other. Costas would come and go with no problem. But Yanni would never let anyone else have visitors. Costas would pick me up on his motorcycle and we would ride off in the night. Actually, he'd just take me for a drink and maybe a strip club if I was lucky. He was tall, dark and handsome with blue eyes (which was unusual for a Greek man). He had a great sense of humor and our relationship was light and fun. We both shared a love for Depeche Mode and he generously gave me the new Depeche Mode tape. Gifts were few and far between. Since he wasn't the wining and dining type, but more the type to take me out for coffee and maybe smoke some hash, I gladly accepted his gift.

He was in the Army and would sneak out to see me at night. I thought that was romantic but would later find out that he was seriously disturbed. One night, we met up and he starting freaking out.

With tears in his eyes, he told me of how they would beat him in the military. I suppose he was anticipating more beatings when he went back. On another occasion, we met up and went to a local bar. I remember stumbling into my room when I returned home and running to the bathroom to throw up. I felt drugged, not drunk, and the club we were at was known to put drugs in drinks. I hadn't drank that much, yet I was so sick. I am sure my aunt heard me but she never said a word. The next day I would get up at the "crack of dawn," as my mom would say, to be in Athens for a job, posing in the glaring sun. Somehow I would look fabulous through it all.

Costas would drop me off at the hotel and there was never a dull moment, always some drama going on when I arrived. Rumors about models and drama would circulate the hotel. Yanni was always yelling about something that was pissing him off, sometimes shouting at his son or his wife. There was also a water shortage in Athens and he was stressing out. But sometimes he would just yell when he was happy. I felt right at home.

I rarely talked to my parents on the phone so I wrote them letters periodically. Once I spoke to my dad and told him I was looking to get my nose pierced. "If you pierce your nose, don't come home," he threatened.

So one Sunday we went to the flea market and I found a street vendor to do it. I'm not even sure what happened, it was so fast. Getting my nose pierced next to a guy selling nuts probably wasn't the best idea. But it turned out fine. Conveniently my Godparents had a jewelry shop by Yanni's and I dropped by to show them my piercing. They gladly gave me a diamond stud to wear and I was set.

03/1/1993

Mom,

Just a quick note- I'm so happy living here in Athens. I've made some good friends in the hotel and it's so relaxing. I stop by Aunty Eleni's sometimes but not for long. My boyfriend drops me by to pick up more of my stuff. I might stay there one night this week. In thirty days Athens will have no water. Already my boyfriend's town has no water. His town is next to Glyfada. I don't know what everyone is going to do. I guess the models will think twice about leaving the water running and the lights on when they go out just to piss Yanni off.

They're having a lot of dinners lately for the models. I mean really nice dinners. Not pizza and salad like before.

Well, I finally got an editorial. It's not great but I can use some of it. It looks more catalog. I think I'm becoming the catalog queen here. But my book has really improved. This photographer that did the editorial job with me is really nice and works for Elle magazine and wants to test me for free!   Just the fact that I got the connections with the photographer from "Elle" is good for me.   I mean they don't use the models here for Elle usually unless they have amazing books and are just passing through but it's good for him to know who I am. And he'll have the test pictures of me and the job. He can always make suggestions. I'm still debating on switching agencies but I'm scared. It just doesn't look good.

Bye for now,

Love Zoe

THE WILD ROSE

The pollution was horrible in Athens. I was constantly sick with a cold or infection and starting to think of a way to get out of the city for a while. Going back to Glyfada was an option (where the house was close to the beach and the air was cleaner) but I really just wanted to get out of Greece for a while. I had met a young French model after a brief break up with Costas, but even he wasn't worth staying for. So I talked to my agency about sending me to Milan.

04/1/93

Mom and dad,

Just a quick note to keep you updated. I should be leaving for Milan in about three days. I'm taking the bus. They should pay for a hotel / apartment there. I'll probably only be there maybe one – two weeks because it's really hard to work. But I'm taking advantage of it because in Milan they take good care of you and you get free tests so I will have a great book when I leave. I think Stavros is trying to get Eleni to advance me a ticket to Milan to work there. Things are never guaranteed in this business. But in Milan I do know that they like to make stars and you are taken care of very well. I'll be glad to get out of

Athens. I've been sick ever since I've lived in this city. I know I've taken care of myself. But the pollution is horrible. I see people with masks on and I have coughing attacks on the streets. I'm sure taking the bus doesn't help because you might as well be kissing the person in front of you. You're so close- squashed in like sardines. Or the guy behind you is rubbing his legs against you.

I'm sure when I get back to the states you will think I've become very aggressive. I just get so sick of the way they treat foreigners here. One time I called a taxi at the hotel because I had to be at a client's place immediately. They especially wanted to see me. The area wasn't on the map they gave me. So the taxi comes and on our way there I'm trying to tell him the address. And he has no idea what I'm talking about. So I made him take me back to Yanni's and had Yanni explain to him. So finally he had to talk to the agency on the phone. Well by the time we left the meter was on 500 drachmas ($2). I told Yanni I wasn't going to pay it and he said it was my problem. Well, I was so late I couldn't afford to lose this taxi. So we go and of course after driving around in circles for half an hour and asking about fifteen people where it was we found it. Well, I argued with the taxi driver forever I was not going to give him 1,500 drachmas ($14) so he could get lost and make me late. The client saw the taxi and came out probably thinking I was looking for his address. So the client is standing *outside the taxi and I'm screaming at the taxi driver in English and he's screaming at me in Greek and finally I just threw a 1,000 drachmas ($4) at him and slammed the door. And he was swearing at me as I walked away. Finally he screeched away. The client just stood there in awe. No wonder I didn't get the job.*

Keep in touch,

Love Zoe

We were invited to a club in Athens for dinner. It wasn't unusual for the clubs to bribe the models with free food and liquor because it would bring them more business. The models sucked it up as most of us were starving, financially and physically. They fed us pizza and then pumped us with alcohol as they watched in amusement while the models got drunk and embarrassed themselves.

The Stereo MC's were playing "Connected" and I locked eyes with this boy wearing a colorful Rastafarian looking sweatshirt. He was magnificent. He had blondish shoulder length hair that fell across his face and blue eyes that I could drown in. As he towered over me, I fell victim to his French accent and all bets were off. We laughed and flirted while I barely understood a thing he was saying. The next thing I knew he picked me up with his big, strong arms, threw me over his shoulders and carried me out of the club. When we stumbled into his models hotel, I needed to use the restroom. He directed me and I felt my way in the dark to the bathroom. When I came out, I went into what I thought was his bedroom. I tried to get into bed and a man yelled in a Greek accent, "What are you doing?

Embarrassed, I said "Oh excuse me!"

I had accidentally walked into the owner's room instead of Jordan's, my new French boyfriend. Quickly sobering up after waking up the owner, I finally found him.

We went out on a couple of dates, which meant I bought myself a beer in his company and hung out at the clubs.

Summer was approaching and the models were leaving town, as work was known to be scarce during these months, although the agencies would say the opposite to keep you there. It was getting hot and I was ready for a break. My agency told me they would set me up in Italy with an agency. So I got a ticket for a ferry going to Rome to then catch a bus in Milan. I was so excited to be going to Milan, especially since I was broke and they were going to take care of things, or so I thought. I took $50 with me and prayed for the best.

When I got on the ferry, I was sick. It must have been a school holiday because there were a million teenagers and they were all sea sick. I was already sick with the flu, so listening to students throwing up constantly made me even sicker. I laid on a bench and prayed for better days. This was not a good start to my trip and would indeed set the precedence.

When we got to the port, I got on the bus and sat next to an older gentleman. He spoke a little English so I told him where I was going. We discussed the fact that I was only carrying $50 in my pocket and he looked concerned. I told him that they were going to pay for my room in Milan and I would figure out the rest when I got there. Sadly, the money had dwindled when we stopped off at a sandwich place and I spent about $20 on a sandwich. My theory, "spend now worry later" was in full effect. When we got to Milan he handed me some cash. He must have foreseen the disaster approaching. He must have been an angel. My Italian angel.

"Who are you again?" the lady with an Italian accent said on the phone.

"My name is Zoe, I am from Talent Models. They sent me."

"Hold on please."

"Hello?" I said a little worried.

"Hello?"

"Yes, Zoe, I am sorry but we have no information on you."

"But they said you had the information and that you would put me in a room."

"No, I am sorry. I don't have any information. We can find you a room but you will need to pay."

I sunk into my jacket and dropped my suitcase. Still recovering from the flu, shaking, I hung up the phone.

I was back at my Aunt's house only a few hours, still sick, but I needed to let off some steam. So I unpacked an outfit and went to my favorite night club in Athens, The Wild Rose, where I was a regular. I was now their celebrity customer as most of the models had left town for the summer. I would walk up to the ropes and they would let me in right away. I would quickly say hello to the kitchen staff, maybe pose for a picture and then work my way to the end of the club where it was elevated. The remaining models and I would look down at the people dancing as we drank for free.

Once I sat with Carlos Salvador, the famous American actor, I encountered at a club before, on the highest level as he threw back whiskey shots and we argued about all the women surrounding him. I thought it was cheap. He was known to enjoy his share of prostitutes and he expected the women at the club to go home with him. We fought about my "morals and values" as if he cared. He came back later around 4 o'clock in the morning and shook my hand, "No hard feelings, yeah?" he said. I gave him a crooked fake smile. He had after all offered me a Tylenol when I told him I had a headache earlier on in the night.

Or maybe I thought it was Tylenol? I wondered.

I was, ignorantly, trying to convince a famous actor that prostitutes and whiskey were not morally correct even though it seemed to be clearly working for him.

As I sipped on my drink, I saw a friend and headed towards her. When I got closer, I recognized the guy she was with. Jordan! By the look on his face, I had just caught him with his hand in the cookie jar (as they say in America) and I smelled a big fat French rat. Surprise!

"Muuuu, wt agh yu doin uhh ere?" He said. "But...uhhh... I thought you wegh een Meelan? No?"

"No, I came back," I said staring blankly at him and his date, my so-called "friend."

I stormed out, furious as Jordan chased after me.

"Zoe, uhhh, wait, uhhh, I can explain uhhh!"

"Explain what? I was only gone for a couple days and you're with my friend?"

"Yes, but uh... uh... I could uh, not elp eet, she came to me..." blah blah blah blah.

Bye bye friend. Au 'revoir Jordan.

Years later I was bartending in South Beach and he walked up to the bar where I worked and gave me a heart attack. I let him have it all over again.

LETTERS TO MOM AND DAD

PARANOIA

I moved back to Glyfada to the house where I spent many summers as a child with Yia Yia. I had such great memories there of when my cousins and I would go down to the plateau and get on the bus to go to the beach.

We'd stay at the beach all day, sipping on Coke out of a glass bottle and eating homemade sandwiches, with the smell of Coppertone in the air. Tired, after spending all day there, we'd get back on the bus to come home amidst the smell of armpit. From the smell of the ocean to the smell of B.O. We would be sun burnt and ready for a nap. When we got home, we'd sit around the table and eat watermelon like it was our last meal. After we took showers and washed ourselves in the boudoir, we would get ready for siesta.

The whole town would sleep for two hours in the afternoon. It was like the world had shut off for those two hours. The phone didn't ring, the lights off, with just the sound of the fans blowing. Then we would wake up to the smell of my Grandmother's cooking. She often made Pastichio and Moussaka. The cream sauce on the top would make me gag so I would scrape it off and eat the rest. Knowing how offended my Yia Yia would be, I would just feed it to the dogs under the table. They were ready and willing. In the evenings, we would sit on the swing outside our bedrooms, smelling the gardenias in full bloom and watching the neighborhood while chatting about boys. Not a care in the world.

Now I was twenty-two, and the little girl in me yearned for her Yia Yia. The house was full of people, the phone ringing, neighbors visiting, just like it was growing up. But without Yia Yia, there was an emptiness. She was always cooking for the dogs, Bully and Bella. They slept outside but would try to sneak in through the kitchen door. She'd yell at them,

"Get out of here!"

They would run outside and wait anxiously for their food. She adored them but having two dogs as pets was not normal in those days. The only dogs around were street dogs that would hang around the Tavernas waiting for a tourist to feed them a scrap.

Now I felt my Yia Yia watching over me as I slept in the library in the house. The summer months were slow and I needed to save money so I stayed there. Somehow I got a job working in a night club called Paranoia. The manager and his girlfriend took a liking to me and would pick me up on their way to work. When we got there I would go into the kitchen and make Frappes for everyone, the coffee drink was similar to drinking liquid crack. I would dose out 2-3 spoons of coffee and 2-3 spoons of sugar, mix it so that there was foam on the top (like a cappuccino), add ice and then milk. And off we went, like rockets blasting into space.

The job was easy. The Greeks tended to drink mostly scotch on the rocks unlike the Americans, who were more complicated with their cocktails, like the Martini. When I bartended in America and was asked to make a Martini it would be preceded with the game "Twenty Questions." Shaken or stirred? On the rocks or straight up? Olives? Onions? Dry or with Vermouth?

The Greeks were simple. It was either on the rocks or neat and drinks were always followed with water. They knew how to get drunk and they knew how to sober up. So I served a lot of Chivas, Dewar's, and Ballantines.

I was living with my aunt, uncle and two cousins. One cousin, Chrisanthe, had epilepsy from a skating accident so she frequently had seizures. Her health was at risk, as the mystery of her seizures could not be solved or cured with medication. I was told not to let her drink. But she wasn't listening to anybody, especially me. The other cousin, Valerie was in love so she spent all her time with her boyfriend. We were close and shared the same birthday. I didn't have brothers or sisters but she would be the closest to one. Although she was much younger, I felt a connection with her. I would end up being the example that every mother would wish for by sharing a joint with her and taking her to McDonald's. I knew how to win someone over, get them stoned and then feed them strawberry shakes and French fries. I thought of myself as carefree, free spirited and just plain fun. I was the crazy, fun cousin not the boring college student that I almost fell victim to. Who had time to study when they could have my life?

My aunt was cool. She never tried to tell me what to do. I came and went as I pleased, sometimes giving her money to hang on to for me. She kept to her business and stayed out of mine offering to help when she could. She was in mourning since she had lost her mother, my Yia Yia, and was always rescuing some sort of animal. Trying to nurse them back to health and stay close to them, she'd push them around the house inside a shopping cart. The little creatures hanging on to life, depending on her as she made sure she was at their beck and call. She was always dressed in black and the smell of incense would follow her as she lit candles all over the house. When she left, she would lock her bedroom door and I wondered what she had hiding in there.

I slept in the library next to an old piano still there from when I was a child. My aunt was remodeling her house upstairs and I'd be woken up by the sounds of drilling in the morning. Between the yelling and the drilling, it was like World War II. It was strange for me to sleep in the library as I was accustomed to sleeping in my own bedroom when I had lived there many years prior. But my aunt and her family had to live there while their house upstairs was being remodeled.

The library was dusty and old and reminded me of when I was a child playing the piano there. There were books and old records on the shelves. I found myself going through them and found personal journals my father had written while attending University in England. It was hard to believe such a strict father had been a typical student at one time. I guess that's why he was so over protective. He knew what boys were capable of doing because he did it himself.

I also got a job working for Marlboro at the Grand Prix making really good money. On my days off I would take the bus or a taxi to Athens and go to castings from there. I was able to save money and figure out what I was going to do next. I didn't want to stay in the house too long. But it was too slow for me to stay in the hotel too. I had to act fast. So I decided to switch agencies. I left Talent Agency and went to Models 500, where the owner was known to be a bitch but all I cared about was working. While walking around in the agency I noticed Lauren Hutton's composite card on the wall.

Wow, she is beautiful, I thought as I picked up her card. I stared at it and thought to myself, *if she's here, why am I?* My insecurities flooded back.

LETTERS TO MOM AND DAD

04/20/1993

Mom and dad,

Well, I've got a half hour before I have to get ready for work. But tomorrow I have to go to the post office to get your package so I will send you this and a couple of pictures.

Well, I will start off this letter by saying that I've just discovered that since I've been living in this house I've been frying my eggs in the oil that Aunty Eleni uses to burn the candles. So I expect my stomach to blow up or something any minute. This was my schedule last week:

Friday	*9am-6pm - commercials*
	6pm-8pm - Marlboro fitting
	10pm-3am - Paranoia Bar
Saturday	*8am-10pm - Marlboro*
	10pm-5:30am - Paranoia
Sunday	*10am-10pm - Marlboro*
Monday	*4pm-10pm - Marlboro*
Tuesday	*8am-12pm - commercial*
	1am-4am - went out with a friend / pizza for the models
Wednesday	*10pm-4am - Paranoia*

I'm officially a workaholic now! So I worked for Marlboro. Got paid $250 a day (in my pocket) for two days to sit around for about nine hours and smoke all the Marlboro cigarettes I want. I had to dance for a well known Greek singer. I had to dance ten minutes every hour then help out with the games. Anyway, being the ungrateful, selfish person I am according to my first agency I thought that I deserved more than $250 for my hard work so I managed to get my hands on fifteen key chains, four hats, two t-shirts, thirty lighters, fifteen boxes of matches and ten packs of cigarettes.

So Greece is supposed to be really busy for work in May and my agency wants me to stay. I'm happy I switched. My other agency was bullshit. They realized what they lost. And now I'm working OK.

Aunty Eleni, Chrisanthe and I were eating at Ainas and she decided to go all out on the lottery and bought a ton of tickets. She said, "could you imagine four hundred million drachmas? If I won none of us would have to work ever again!" And I said – "none of us work anyway".

Aunty Eleni came home crying today. She hooked Phoenix (her dog) up on an I.V. because she's going to die in a couple days. She has something wrong with her kidneys. I feel so awful. She looks so skinny and sick and tired. It just doesn't seem fair. Phoenix was fine this time last week. Now she's going to die in a couple days.

Anyway, I have to go. Sorry to end my letter like that.

I hate sleeping in the library. It's so creepy. Lately I've been sleeping with Chrisanthe because this house is haunted or something. But I keep getting bit by spiders in the library. Probably because there's food in there.

Anyways, bye

S & M VODKA

When I was bartending in Greece, I got to know my co-workers and they became my friends. They would sometimes recognize me on television from doing a commercial and it would later become a topic for conversation. One of my latest commercials was for an advertisement for mosquito repellent. It wasn't a big acting debut, like the Lottery commercial I did pretending I had just won, where I thought I showed my true acting skills.

This might take me to the next level, I remember thinking.

Little did I know that it was barely considered acting and just one of the duties of a model. For instance, when I was in a Greek music video, just floating around making serious faces. In the mosquito repellent commercial all I did was sit around at a table and play cards with other models. Shooting that commercial, I would end up meeting a man that would be a part of a future job. We worked well together and he would tell me about his wife. The next time I saw him was at Mercedes Night Club in my hometown, Glyfada.

The agency had set up a job for me to promote Smirnoff vodka. I went to get fitted and the outfit looked a little risqué on the hanger. But when I was fitted for the outfit, I thought it was somewhat tasteful. They gave me a mask and a whip but as it was for a major brand like Smirnoff I assumed that it was okay. I didn't put too much thought into it since I knew that it was their trademark at the time. The agency reassured me that I would be just handing out drinks to the customers for a couple hours. When I got there, the plans had clearly changed. I was to perform a show. "A show!" I said. I froze and looked down at my outfit with whip in hand.

How was I going to do this?

The gentleman that I would be performing with in the show was the same model I worked with in the mosquito repellent commercial. So since this news got me completely stressed out, I started drinking the free Smirnoff. If I was going to perform on a stage in Mercedes Night Club I needed to get drunk! I wasn't prepared, mentally or physically.

My partner started hitting on me and I felt very uncomfortable. Little did he know that by hitting on me, he would piss me off so much, it would give me ammunition for the show as I knew he was married. During the commercial he told me all about his wife. One thing I didn't like was a cheater. I had ended a serious relationship back home in Arizona just before coming to Greece because he was cheating on me. I was freshly scorned. This would give me fuel to get me pumped for the show. I was pissed!

The lights came on. Then the music. I felt the energy. I was at the top of the stairs on the stage looking down on the crowd. I saw flashes of light and was blinded which helped because there were a lot of people there that I could not see. The photographers were taking pictures and the crowd was watching, waiting for the ultimate show. So I dragged my slave down the stairs and the crowded room roared with excitement. I pulled him down three or four steps and then pulled him closer to me, as if I was going to kiss him. Then I kicked him and watched him cower and fall down the stairs. The crowd was screaming in delight. I was thrilled. What a rush! I whipped him and kicked him until we got to the bottom. Every push down the stairs was one for the ex. It felt liberating. I was a hit and it was obvious by the response from the crowd that they loved me. When I got to the bottom of the stairs everyone was cheering and yelling. I'm sure my partner was a little more than sore. He looked a little bewildered. We never spoke again. I would later mingle with the people in the club and meet Marcus Schukenberg, who was a male supermodel of that time.

The next day, I went to go visit my aunt. As I sat at the table, my father's best friend came bustling through the door. "I saw you on television. They are talking about you and the night club you performed at," he said.

"What?" I said, embarrassed, but with a smirk on my face. *How could this be? I wasn't paid for that?*

"Yes, you are on a show called Histories of the Wild," he said.

I had a mask on! Oh great, I thought.

My father is going to flip. Later that night, at the bar, my Greek friends came in smirking as they had also seen it. The Greeks were suckers for stuff like that. This job turned out to be innocent fun but the Greek television commercials bordered on soft porn. I can only imagine what they made out of it. Thank God I didn't see it.

MADWORLD

After saving some money I set my sights on Barcelona, Spain. It was there that I would discover the "Chupa Chup," the delicious lollipop that would taste like heaven and bring my roommate and I closer. I stayed in an apartment owned by a gay couple and the agency had arranged for me to stay there with a girl from Miami. The apartment was on the artsy, "Gothic" side of Las Ramblas, next to the Picasso museum. When the taxi dropped me off, he tried to drive down the narrow streets and barely made it through, scraping the side his car. I remember someone telling me that the building was eight hundred years old. I felt like I was a part of the twilight zone, traveling back in time, as I walked along the stone streets. I looked up at the balconies with clothes hanging from some of them. Women peering down, wrinkles on their faces telling stories.

My roommate, Julie, arrived a few days later. She came very early in the morning. When I answered the door, I was half asleep and directed her to the kitchen where she could make herself some coffee. Later, she would tell me that she realized that I was not a morning person from my lack of hospitality. But we eventually became good friends. She didn't look like the average model. She was tall and thin with long, thick, red hair. I thought of her as a Jewish Sophia Loren. She was educated, cultured and well-traveled. She had my sarcastic, witty personality and we spent a lot of time laughing and gossiping about the other models. She also seemed to know many of the male models from Miami and their stories. We frequented a bar called Zig Zag, where I dropped acid for the first time. She was prude when it came to men always keeping them on their toes, but she always knew who gave the best party in town. We played pool and laughed and laughed for hours until our jaws hurt. Playing pool had never been so hilarious as it was that particular night. I still don't know exactly what made it so funny. I'm guessing the party favors contributed.

One night, as we were coming home late from our castings, we heard familiar music echoing through the stone streets. Jane's Addiction was playing from a distance. As we got closer we recognized this American music and became curious. We found the little bar that was hidden like a hole in the wall in the narrow streets. When we entered we were pleasantly surprised to talk to an American bartender. Julie knew Spanish fluently so she was trying to speak Catalan to the bartender. After about two sentences of struggling, he interrupted her and said, "It's OK, I'm American."

We started laughing and ordered some beers. Later we sat around a big table with a few people and smoked hash. Everybody was so open and welcoming as we chatted. When we left, Julie went home and crashed in her bed. She was never one to get the munchies. I walked to the beach and sat looking at the ocean while I contemplated my life, my future, and what I could find to eat. I couldn't believe I was there; it was like being in a dream.

Our agency was called Group Models. A lovely French couple ran it above a restaurant they also owned. They were incredibly nice and would allow the models to eat for free in their restaurant. They were unlike any agency I had ever worked for. They were generous, respectful, honest and pleasant. They never put me down and did their best to find me work and test shoots. They introduced me to a photographer who would take some body shots of me as I was going on a lot of castings for bathing suits but had no body shots. They set me up on various castings and tried to get me work. I would later get some great ones during an editorial for a Spanish magazine.

One day, they set me up to do a free test shoot with an American photographer at his apartment in Barcelona. When I got to his youth hostel that he called an apartment, I was ready to do some lingerie shots for body shots. I had already done a swimsuit shoot with him on the beach so I felt comfortable since I had already worked with him. I must have sent the wrong signals at that shoot by lying out topless that day. It wasn't unusual to lay out topless in Europe so I didn't think twice. When I got to his so called apartment, I asked him where the bathroom was so that I could change. This short little man with stringy long hair started to give me attitude and tell me that if I didn't trust him enough to undress in front of him, the shoot wasn't going to work out. I felt my blood boil. I had come all this way for nothing. Wasted money for the train. How dare he insinuate that he was going to see me naked? I told him to go fuck himself and his shoot and walked out. Although disappointed about not doing the shoot, I felt empowered for all women, especially models, when I left.

Even with that negative experience, Barcelona would become my favorite place in the world. I loved the people and the architecture. Antonio Gaudi became my new favorite architect. The vibrant colors and intense shapes took my breath away. I felt like stepping into one of his buildings and becoming Alice in Wonderland. The people there would do anything to help you, even if they couldn't speak English. I vowed to go back one day, maybe even to live.

The models would meet at Las Ramblas and we would have a drink or get a falafel. Every day in the square there was an endless line of people waiting to buy their falafels and they were worth waiting for. We would go and get our daily fix. Julie and I were trying to save money so we would go and buy bread, tuna and tomatoes and make sandwiches. It seemed to be a popular sandwich there. When we had a little cash we went out for Chinese food. We laughed at ourselves realizing, here we are in Spain, where they had amazing Paella and we are spending our only money on Chinese food.

The models would get together and take the train to a quaint little town called Sitges. We had heard it was artsy, young and gay friendly. I'm not sure why it mattered that it was gay friendly. Perhaps because the stylists and photographers would go also. I felt more comfortable around gays probably because I was so uncomfortable in my own skin growing up that I felt a similarity between us. So we would go and lay out at the beach, topless, frolicking in the beautiful clear water, checking each other out. We didn't have a care in the world while Tears for Fears echoed through the speakers hooked up to the Walkman in the sand.

One day, on our way back on the train, we heard the sky roaring and saw fires in people's back yards. The models looked at each other with confusion. I thought Spain was at war. People were burning their furniture in bonfires and setting off fireworks. When I got off the train, I stood outside and ducked for a minute thinking there was a bomb hitting us it was so loud. We would later find out that Saint Joan was a big holiday in Spain. It symbolized cleansing one's self in which you burned the old and bring yourself good luck. There were parties all night and the buildings shook from the fireworks.

Barcelona had my heart forever. Even my worst day there proved to me how sincere the people were. One day I was going to castings and stopped off at the bank to change some money. When I was on the train I realized that I did not have my book/portfolio. I panicked and couldn't breathe as I searched the immediate area. I took the train back to the bank and it was just about to close. I pounded on the door for them to let me in. When I went inside, I asked if they had seen a book with pictures. Sure enough someone presented it to me. Tears of joy started rolling down my face. I was so grateful to them for keeping it for me. My book was my life. This was the early nineties, not an era of "backing up" your stuff on a hard drive. Everything was on paper and I did not have a copy of my book as was suggested. We had physical negatives not the disks that they have today. My book was to me what a portfolio is to a painter or a computer to a graphic artist. Without my book, I would not work. I truly loved the people and the culture in Spain.

DINE AND DASH

I came back from Barcelona forever changed. I had never felt so alive and free. As I dragged my feet into my Agency, I was told there was not much work coming up, and that the two richest men in Athens were taking the models on a trip to Mykonos. I was encouraged to go and get to know them. My American friend Sasha, who was dating a public relations guy for the clubs, was also going.

I felt comfortable around Sasha because she came from California, a place I frequented in my teens. She was attractive and had been a Vogue cover girl model in many countries so she had a reputation of being a "working model." But she didn't seem to work often now and spent most of her nights with her boyfriend at the clubs partying, convincing us models to go out. She looked tired and drained. One day, I went out to lunch with her and she pulled something I had never tried. We finished our lunch and when the check came, she got up and grabbed my hand and said, "Come on! Let's go!" I was so confused. I told her that we needed to pay. She said we were pulling a "dine and dash." I had no idea what she meant but quickly put it together that my friend was a thief. I felt uncomfortable. These were my people, the Greeks. And they worked hard for their money. Fortunately for me and unfortunately for her, she had left her very expensive jacket on the chair, so we had to go back and pay.

We all set sail to go to Mykonos and I was leery of these rich gigolos and what their expectations were, but I needed a change. The fact that it was free also helped since I had just spent all my money in Spain. I packed my bags and took a taxi to meet Sasha, and we hopped onto the ferry with a bunch of models and the two men, whom I had never met. When we got there, we unpacked and got ready for a night out. The villa was beautiful overlooking the clear turquoise ocean. Sasha and I were in the bathroom and she offered me some white powder. I trusted her and didn't think much of it.

We blasted off into the night. Everything became much clearer. The music was brilliant and the islanders were warm and accommodating. We (the models) spoke for hours over cocktails and danced the night away. Everybody was laughing and I felt so alive again. It took me back to Barcelona. But the night wore off and we sailed back to Athens. I took a taxi from the port alone and walked the rest of the way to my hotel. I missed Julie.

LOOK IT UP!

I spent so many months writing to my parents about my adventures in Greece. Occasionally, we would talk on the phone and every time I mentioned any kind of modeling terminology they would answer with, "yes, yes." When I asked them if they knew what I was talking about, they would say no, laughing under their breath. So I decided to write them definitions of every term I had learned along the way.

08/20/1993

OK Mom and Dad- It's time for you to learn the terms of the modeling business because it seems that when I'm trying to tell you what's going on in my life with modeling you just agree but I don't think you know what the hell I'm talking about. OK.

Shoot - a session of taking pictures with a photographer.

Editorial - a job you get with a magazine. This is the most important type of job a model can get. That is why models go to Europe. It is easier to find editorial work in Europe than the states. In fact there isn't much of a chance of getting many kinds of work - especially editorial in the United States without having editorial tear sheets in your book. Because everyone wants editorial work it *pays really bad. You can get paid $100-$200 at the most for the cover of Vogue magazine. But it's an investment you make to work more.*

Tear Sheet- a picture you got paid to do. You can have editorial tear sheets, catalog tear sheets, or advertisement tear sheets. A good model should only have tear sheets in her book, rather than test pictures because it proves that she works. But to be able to get tear sheets you have to prove to the client that you are photogenic so you need test until then.

Tests - every model has to start out with test. When a photographer "tests" you there really is no guarantee that the pictures will turn out amazing unless he's John H. or something. But you keep testing until you find something good enough to show clients that you are photogenic.

Booking - a job (confirmed).

Composite Card - a laser card or a real card. My first card was a real composite (although it was poor because it had no color pictures and only one tear sheet on it). Because most models in Europe are always coming and going they are always using laser cards (what I sent you). Every time you enter a different market you have to change your composite because every market is looking for different looks and pictures.

For example - Spain likes editorial and catalog looks, Germany likes catalog looks and NY and L.A. like editorial. Greece does not know what the hell they want. In my case, I might have not done so well in Spain because they do a lot of bathing suit and lingerie catalog. I have nothing like that in my book. But I tested here and got some nice stuff. It's a pity I didn't test as soon as I got here.

Market - every country has a different market. When one market isn't working for you- you move to the next market.

Book - portfolio. A model's book is like a pilot's airplane. Without it he can't go anywhere. Your book is your resume. It shows where you've been, what you've done and where you're going. If it is full of tests, it shows that you have no experience. If it's full of tear sheets, it shows that you've probably been working for years. If your tear sheets are from shitty magazines like Woman's Guide or Phoenix Houses it shows you have potential but you could do better. In that case you can't work for a big paying client and you have to settle for an average life. If you have tear sheets from Vogue, Elle, and catalog of big designers you can get filthy rich.

Modeling - modeling is an investment. You go to college for four years and get a degree. Then you start getting paid according to how experienced you are. You start a profession and you build your resume. A real model goes to Europe for at least two years to build her book. She gets paid according to her experience. Then you build your book and the stronger it gets the better the jobs will be. Then when you get back to the states your hourly rate doubles because you have been to Europe. When you're in college, you can only get a real job after you get that piece of paper that says you are qualified. It's the same in modeling. You're qualified after you go to Europe. After you've been to Europe (mainly Germany, Paris, and Milan) your career should rise. Then after working maybe two years in the states, if your book is strong enough you can have a daily rate of $1,000-$5,000.

So - I'm back in Greece - got a letter from you (nothing at the agency). Bye for now.

Love Zoe

SEPTEMBER

Although I was glad that I switched agencies, the owner of the new one was really a bitch. She was abrupt and controlling. But I had to listen to her because she was the one getting me the work. It made me realize how pleasant everyone was at my agency in Arizona. People were so different in the States.

I was missing my family more and more. I missed the simple things like just watching westerns on television with my dad or going shopping at the mall with my mom. I missed the coffee shops where I would hang out with my friends and listen to poetry readings and bands play. That would be unheard of in Athens. I missed my bed and my room most of all. I forgot how easy I had it living at home, listening to my stereo and going to parties with my old college friends. I missed my mom's cooking and had forgotten what it was like to have a home cooked meal. I also missed my model friends who were humble compared to the models in Athens.

Even the castings were different in Athens. There were models from all over the world and the competition seemed so tough. The English and German models were really serious and professional. The few Greek models kept to themselves and the American models liked the night life but always made the castings. Some of them were just passing through and had amazing books, full of tear sheets. It sometimes made me feel inadequate. The clients would flip through my book having made a decision at "Hello." Going to castings was constantly challenging my self-esteem, whether I didn't feel tall enough, skinny enough, or pretty enough. The client had a specific idea of what they were looking for and it wasn't always me. But it also made me stronger and prepared me for the market in Arizona.

9/14/1993

Mom and Dad

I really miss everyone and I want to come home! I'm OK really – so I have a little aggression in me and I haven't slept for three days.

You can't imagine how hard it is trying to be a model. Everyone thinks they know more than you or they are better than you. Sometimes they just don't give me a chance. Everyone says the owner of my agency is such a bitch. And she is. They want me to get cards. It is really cheap here but I'm trying to get out! They don't want me to leave because they are making so much money off of me. And where's all my money going? Back to them because I'm investing it all in modeling. Now that it's September the clients could give a shit about me because there are so many new models in town.

LETTERS TO MOM AND DAD

Our house has as much life as a monastery. Aunty Eleni is alone a lot. But she spends all her time reviving little kittens. One died. Now we have a two week old black kitten with a blue eye. I think her life is about visiting sick people and bringing animals back to life. Yesterday somebody put a dog at our front door with a plate of food and water. I think our neighbors are just sending strays to our house. But Aunty Eleni refused to pay any attention to the dog. It was so cute. Dad, this morning it was gone.
I miss you,

Love Zoe

LETTERS TO MOM AND DAD

JULIE

I talked to Julie on the phone and convinced her to come to Greece to model. She stayed with me at the house for a night but there was so much noise going on upstairs due to the construction it was not what she had in mind. So we both moved back to Yanni's.

09/25/1993

Mom and Dad,

Well, it's 11:00 at night and everybody's asleep and all is quiet except that Aunty Eleni is up of course wandering the house. My light was off and she thought I was asleep. But I can't sleep because Julie is coming. Anyway, it is not uncommon for people to wander in and out of my bedroom all day seeing as the food in in here. Chrisanthe comes in at 6:00 am to feed her cat and Aunty Eleni at night to feed her cat., etc. so I thought I'd scare the shit out of Auntie Eleni tonight since I haven't had a good laugh in a while. She was knelt down with her head in the cupboard. Swearing about how there was no food for the animals. I thought about doing something but I didn't want her to hit her head on the cupboard. So I waited until she got up. Now she thought I was fast asleep since the light was off and I didn't move. But she thought wrong because I jumped up in my bed and screamed "boo!" I scared her so bad she looked like she was gonna piss her pants. So she almost dropped what she was holding and jumped and then said "Just you wait until Dimitri comes tomorrow!" Now for anybody to tell me that is like saying to me "grab the earplugs and run," because for the past few days I have gotten up at six in the morning to the sound and feeling that the ceiling was going to land on me. Not to mention my eyes swollen almost shut and my body broken out in hives from all the dust. I think it's time to move for a while. I think I will stay at Yanni's for a few weeks (3 or 4) then move back here and work at the bar full time when modeling gets slow again.

Anyway, tonight I came to the conclusion that the Greek blood in me is slowly showing through the American I thought I was. I realized that for the past two weeks straight I've been eating salad every day. Not just any salad, mind you. Not even a traditional Greek salad. I'm talking a real down to earth Greek salad. Simple- that's it. I'm talking tomatoes, cucumber, green pepper, salt, lots of olive oil and a tad of vinegar, about ten black olives and a big piece of bread to soak up the remaining oil and feta cheese. I realized another thing about the Greek nature in me. Taking a shower every other day is becoming more of a chore and not a luxury. I'm beginning to go three days. What next? Is my Greek blood taking over the American in me? I'm getting worried. That's why it's a good idea that I come home soon. Tomorrow I'm picking up my coupon you sent me and calling TWA to book my ticket. I mean come on. This is how it usually starts. For an alcoholic it's a slow process. Maybe a drink on the weekends. Then getting drunk on the weekends. Then drinking during the week. Before you know it he needs a shot of whiskey when he wakes up every morning. It was a slow process for me as well. First I was forced to speak a little Greek. Second, I was constantly around Greek food. Then I started working at a Greek bar, then before I know it I started listening to Greek music. I think the Greek in me took over when I started doing Greek music videos. Then before you know it I had a Greek boyfriend. That changed a lot of things. Let me just tell you that the Greek guys are just little charmers. What next? A Greek mother-in-law? That's all I need.

Anyways, just thought I'd drop a line- give my love to everyone.

Love Zoe

Julie and I went to castings although they were few and far between because it was slow. She quickly realized the Greeks were not as professional as the Spanish. There would be no agency offering the models free lunch whenever we wanted like in Spain. And the clients weren't as nice. But she enjoyed the change of scenery and I took her around Athens. We enjoyed going to the market by the Acropolis on the weekends, laughing at all the shop owners trying to convince us into go into their stores.

I later introduced her to my boyfriend's friend and we all went out for coffee in Athens. They seemed to like each other and we made plans to go to my hometown and meet one night.

10/01/1993

Dad,

I just want to tell you something that happened yesterday that sent Julie and me into hysterics.

It has been really slow here and we had one casting at the agency. They gave us one more to go to but it was for a Greek music video and they made it sound sort of like "if we wanted to go we could go." So, knowing that it's so slow, we decided to go for the hell of it. Hey $150 for a ten hour commercial is shitty but $150 is $150, so we went. Nobody's there (no models) and we're sitting there and they're ignoring us. Finally they call Julie in but the lady is laughing on the phone flipping through Julie's book. After five minutes of this lady talking on the phone and not even paying any attention to Julie or her book, Julie got up and snatched her book back and walked out. I didn't *even bother showing my book (besides they knew me because I had worked for them two times already). So we left pissed off.*

In the street, we met a guy who we asked if he worked there so we could complain. He said yes. We told him how unprofessional they were being and asked him if there had even been a casting schedule at the office for a job (like the agency had told us). Listen to what he said. "I don't know anything. I'M JUST THE DIRECTOR". We just busted out laughing. I'm sorry dad- as much as I love Greece (and I am proud to have a Greek name) I think it is the most fucked up country in Europe. They don't know what they're doing!

Gotta go, talk soon

Love Zoe

The elections were going on in Greece, and Athens was buzzing with loud horns and cars with people yelling out the windows. I had never seen so much yelling and honking. The younger people were the loudest and we couldn't help but stare. Of course the Greeks loved a good looking woman staring at them and mistook it for something else. Something they called "Kamaki."

Whenever someone hit on us, Julie and I would pretend to not speak English. It started to feel like harassment so we took measures into our own hands and pretended to pick our noses. It didn't really deter them though. They would still hit on us while we walked to our castings.

Work was slow for both of us, especially Julie but she didn't get discouraged. We just made the best of it. I was starting to get tired of the ten hour days for catalog and felt like I was being taken advantage of. But I was still a new model and had to take what I could get. I envied the models that would just come into town for a few days for a job. Some would turn down jobs because of the money. But I couldn't. I needed the tear sheets and experience. I was looking forward to going back to Arizona where things were more professional.

Even though I felt taken advantage of, I was very proud of myself for becoming self-sufficient and independent. I had built my book and now I knew how to move in front of the camera. I had been in many commercials and Greek music videos. I had struggled many times in Arizona with my lack of confidence in front of the camera. But now I felt good. I was a real model. The agency in Arizona would no longer lower my fees because I was new. I had gone to Europe, gained experience and tear sheets and I would get paid accordingly.

Not only was I proud of how hard I had worked in Greece, I was also proud that I had managed to live on my own away from my parents. I had struggled with trying to move out of my parents' house in Arizona. No job would afford me that and my parents weren't exactly pushing me to leave. In Greece, it's not uncommon for adult children to live with their parents. But I wanted independence. I just couldn't do it financially. So now I proved to them that it was possible and that I was a responsible, hardworking adult.

10/14/1993

Dad,

My roommate Julie says that when the Greeks came out of their mother's womb they weren't slapped on the bottom. They were honked at. I think for the last three days of the election every Greek here had their hand super glued to their horn twenty four hours a day. The election here is like a holiday. A fiesta. It was the Greeks goal (not to prove who could run their country the best) to see how many flags they could hook on to their cars, how many people they could stuff in their sunroof, how drunk they could get and who had the loudest horn.

So, to change the subject, Julie and I have decided that every time a Greek comes up to us asking "do you know where the Acropolis is?" or you - me - coffee or does any form of Kamaki (hitting on us), we both stick our fingers in our noses and pick it and look straight at them. It works too. And dad, where did this inspiration come from? Your letter of course. Well, my weight got down to 116 lbs (53 kilos) and I decided that it was time to eat a decent meal so Julie and I went out to dinner. Of course there's no kitchen here. Yanni closed it because supposedly the models were leaving the stove on all the time. I just think it's another excuse to save electricity.

Last night I watched MTV for the first time in ten months. I felt so lost, so uneducated in all that is going on in the world of music.

The American guys we met must have thought I was a real imbecile because when I started asking questions about the news in America they informed me that Clinton was elected president.

Lately it has been really slow and lots of models are here and I'm not getting along with the owner of my agency (which could hinder things a bit). To be honest with you – this is really sad- but unless you hang out with the two richest guys in Greece (Yanni and Dimitri) and go to the islands and party with them, work can get really slow because all the bimbos they hang out with get the important jobs. And there's no work for the struggling models who would like to leave Greece with a bit of dignity.

Anyway, I went all the way to Nea Kiffisias this morning to be at a job at eight am. As usual the clothes didn't come until nine thirty and we hadn't even started make-up or hair. By ten, they decided there was a problem with the clothes matching the backdrop in the studio so they postponed the job until Thursday. We will still get paid for our time though. The other model refused to work for them again (says it's a waste of her *time). She's a big model from N.Y. She's really sweet. But she lives in N.Y. and gets paid $1,500 a day sometimes. She's been doing this for years, has an amazing book and spent three years in Europe. Now it's paying off. So, one day I will come here and turn down these jobs where I get paid 30,000 drachmas ($1,200) for eight hours (editorial) and tell them (the agency) not to waste my time but until then I will work my ass off (even for shitty jobs) until I get there.*

The first six months I was here I was beginning to wonder if it was worth it (coming to Greece). But now I don't regret it one bit. I'm doing well. I've got some really nice stuff coming out. My book is already completely different.

Well dad, I think I did pretty well for myself here. I've completely taken care of myself. I've lived on my own on and off for five months, one month in Spain. I worked reasonably well for a foreign model staying here over six weeks. I've learned to budget my money better! I've got a job on the side for pocket money (to eat, go to castings, buy cards...etc.) and I'm flying myself home and I won't come home without enough money to cover my previous bills.

Everything is so up in the air for me. I want to know what the future holds but I don't and now I'm feeling really good about the modeling. I've finally realized that I'm not just a pretty face and showing up to my jobs thinking that my pretty face is all I need to get paid is wrong. It takes a lot more. If I want to work for the same client and get people interested in me I have to show a professional attitude and really move well and put all my effort into it. It's hard. I mean- you're really working. I guess I didn't realize how hard it was. I had this view that modeling was glamorous with all the free stuff we get and the treatment and the money. But the money just doesn't come like this. My agency is bargaining with the client and if the client pays me more money than usual then he expects a more professional model right? And I have to prove myself. And here I go on babbling.

Anyway, I have to go and send this otherwise if I keep stopping and writing more a few days later, you'll never get this. So − take care. I miss you I can't wait to come home!

Love, Zoe

I enjoyed having Julie as my roommate in Greece. We got along great. She had a great sense of humor and we had so much fun together. One day I took her to visit my boyfriend's friend whom we had already had coffee with in Athens. We took a taxi to Glyfada and I met up with Costas.

He took us to go see his friend who was working in a strip club as a bouncer. That should have been a red flag for us right there and then but I thought he was cute. He had a tough, dangerous, rockabilly style and a chiseled body. We all decided to go back to his house and party. When we got there it smelled like moth balls. Costas had told me that his parents had left because of him. Yet another red flag. Parents don't just get up and leave their own house one day and leave their son unless there is something seriously wrong! So since the smell didn't seem to bother us we stayed. At one point Julie and I were in the bathroom and he came in and started to get rough and forced himself on her. We started yelling while trying to escape the bathroom. We ran out of the house and he chased us down the street in his underwear. We were yelling help and running as fast as we could. It was one of the scariest moments I had ever had. The next day Julie was on the phone with her dad and got a plane ticket home. I was disappointed but understood.

Our room felt empty with her gone and I decided to move back to Glyfada with my Aunt. It was just a matter of time before I needed to go back to the United States. I could only stay in Greece one year with my Green Card and my time was almost up. I was ready to come home. I was coming to terms with how unprofessional people were there. I had built my book and that's what I was there to do. I had achieved my goals both professionally and personally.

11/05/1993

Mom and dad,

Well, I'm sitting here all alone in my room. Julie left this morning back to Miami. She was very disappointed with Greece. She was here six weeks and worked once for a hair show. All the models are leaving Greece because it is so slow. This sucks. She was my best friend here. I don't really have anybody else except for my Greek boyfriend. But he's just my boyfriend. He's not my friend. No he's OK I just can't figure the Greek guys out. But I like him because he reminds me of dad. The way he gets so excited about silly things and starts shouting. And I laugh and then he gets even more excited ranting and raving. The killing look in his eyes when I answer back to him and the way he has to control himself. I especially like it when we get in a fight and he feels guilty so he makes me kiss him on the cheek. And if I don't because I'm pouting or something he is insulted beyond belief. But he's always playing jokes on me and teasing me. And it reminds me of dad.

I can't wait to come home. A South African agency came to Greece and is interested in me coming in January. It's very good money because of the German clients. I think my agency here is going to try and push me to go because the owner said "Oh you can go there for January and February and then come back here to Greece." So if they advance me to go to South Africa I'll go and then come back to Greece. But there's no way I'm staying more than five to six weeks here. You won't catch me staying here another whole year. No way!!

So we'll see what they say. I just sent them my book. I'm getting ready to send the agency in Arizona my tests and tears (if you don't know what that means look it up!) so they can send it out to clients before I get home. I'm not going to make cards because I might come back to Europe straight away and everyone here uses laser cards since the markets are always changing. Germany has been calling my agency here saying they have options (look it up!) in Germany. But unless I'm confirmed a booking (look it up!) there I won't go. If I go to any market I want to at least make enough money to cover the money I invested in the trip.

I want to get out of Greece for a while. This is a dirty business as it is but Greece I think is one of the most screwed up markets. It pays shit and it's mostly who you know or sleep with to get work. I guess it's always like that in all businesses but it wasn't like that in Phoenix. John H. was the best photographer in Arizona and he not only did my book for free but he was patient and professional and considerate. Let's just say if the models have problems with the photographers they won't talk because the next time they come back to Greece they won't work. Thank God I never had a problem here. But I did in Spain. A photographer told me that I wasn't professional and I didn't trust him as a photographer because I wouldn't change in front of him. So I told him to fuck off and walked out of the shoot.

Anyway, enough of the depression. Only five more weeks until I come home! Maybe sooner. But don't think so because I've got some connections in Glyfada- it's just that I'm being my own picky self. But I guess money is money. If I can't bring gifts home for Christmas I will definitely bring chocolates! And Branston Pickle! The first week I come home all I want to do is go thrift shopping and rent fifty million movies and eat Jack in the Box mini chimichangas and anything that I can microwave and just eat and live like a pig. I just need to get it out of my system. Then I'll be OK. Then I'll be back to my normal self. You're probably thinking "what normal self? That's the way you've always been!" Don't worry I've changed a little. Washing my clothes by hand for a year, flushing the toilets with left over water and eating bread and chocolate spread for breakfast, lunch and dinner every day can change a person you know!

Well mom, I received your letter. I was surprised that it wasn't on the cheesy cat cards you keep sending. I know you only write on them because 1. you can't write much so you don't have to worry about writing me on a whole page letter block 2. you're trying to get rid of those horrible cards! I did see that you're still using the other paper I gave you (that you're probably also trying to get rid of)! If I gave you Laura Ashley paper would you write a letter to me on it? I don't think so!

They had a party here at the clubs for the American models for Halloween but I couldn't be bothered. It's not the same. Apparently, most of the people that went were the gay stylists here and they just dressed up as women (of course). One time, Julie and I and Costas (my boyfriend) and his friend went to the clubs and two stylists were trying to pick up on them (Costas and his friend). I was in a taxi with the two stylists and Costas was on his bike with his friend. I made it clear that Costas was my boyfriend but they wouldn't listen. One even jumped out of the taxi and got on the bike with Costas and his friend. When we got to the club I told Costas that they were gay and he wanted to kill them. But I told him to keep his cool and he just stepped on one of the guy's foot.

Well, there's not much news. There are boxes up to the ceiling in this house. There's a small pathway they made with the boxes from the kitchen hallway to my bedroom. It's a real live maze in our house! The house upstairs is going to be beautiful. They are working on it every day. Uncle Claude seems to be in a bad mood because of his working conditions in the house. What working conditions?! You can't move in there. He can't organize his stuff. Aunty Eleni gets home today then I suppose she'll be off to see you guys in a few days. I'd love to come with her. But I think I should wait until at least the 15th of December.

Anyway, see you soon!

Love, Zoe

THE ALPHA & THE OMEGA

The taxi pulled up to my Yia Yia's house and it was finally the end of my journey. I opened the front gate and dragged my luggage down each step, scuffing my suitcase. As the gate slammed shut, my heart ached a little. I looked back and saw myself on the balcony swinging in the chair when I was seven. I was sun burnt and my best friend, Anne from England was sitting next to me. We were gossiping about my cousins and laughing, talking about the boys we met at the beach that day. I saw my Great Dane Sophie barking at the neighborhood kids that were throwing rocks at her. My mom warned them but they didn't listen so she opened the gate and Sophie chased them all the way to the cinema at the end of the street. I heard my Yia Yia yelling at Bully and Bella to get out of the kitchen. I could still smell her fragrance, Chanel #5, that she wore when she went out. Her kind eyes asking my mom why I was crying when I couldn't bear to tell her how much I hated the porridge she fed me before school. I remembered playing the piano in the library where I had spent many nights this past year.

I certainly would not miss that library, I thought.

My cousins and my aunt and uncle stood there as my luggage was put into the trunk. As I got into the taxi outside my house, my cousin Valerie was standing in the middle of the street watching, with tears in her eyes.

What a year this had been, I thought.

Besides modeling and finally spreading my wings, I got to know my cousins like sisters. This was my family. We only knew each other as children spending our summers together before I moved to the states. Now we were adults and were getting to know each other all over again. We went out dancing and came home late and they would visit me at the models hotel in Koukaki. I can still hear the DJ playing Maxi Priest while we dirty danced at a local bar laughing and carrying on, loving all the attention.

We had late night food binges after coming home from work a little tipsy, chatted about boyfriends and my modeling jobs over bread, taramasalata, olives and feta cheese.

I finally felt a part of an extended family as the only family I had in the states were my parents. I felt sadness and relief. I felt empty because I knew it would be a long time before I came back and saw them again. It was a simple life there and I appreciated it but it was a culture that was behind. There was so much that needed to be fixed in Greece and it seemed like it would be an eternity before any changes were made. I felt sadness for the people I was leaving behind, not just my family, but the people I had met on my journey. They didn't have the opportunities I had, nor would they ever. I felt relief because I missed the luxuries that

America had to offer such as a car, hot water, pizza and big shopping malls.

Most of all I felt complete. I had finally proven to myself that I was self-sufficient, that I could handle life on life's terms, and that I could take responsibility for myself.

This was the end of one journey and the beginning or another. I was free.